"I don't

"I need to know your rules for this situation, Signor Corelli. You have rules for everything else. So let me have them."

Dominic cleared his throat. "All right, I make it a rule never to get romantically involved with anyone I'm working with. In my opinion it adds an unwanted level of stress to the workplace." He turned and bent low to whisper in her ear, "But in your case I'm willing to make an exception."

Dominic's mouth descended upon hers and she instinctively wrapped her arms around his neck and pulled him closer. Their mouths hungrily devoured each other and the ache that both of them had been suffering for the past two and a half hours finally eased.

Never in his wildest dreams had Dominic thought a kiss could be this powerful. And he considered himself somewhat of an expert on the subject. It was so intense that as he was kissing her he found that the longer their mouths were locked in the act, the more he wanted. He could go on kissing her and never get enough.

Books by Janice Sims

Kimani Romance

Temptation's Song

JANICE SIMS

is an author of seventeen novels and has had stories included in nine anthologies. She is a recipient of the Emma Award for her novel *Desert Heat* and two Romance in Color awards. She also received an Award of Excellence for her novel *For Keeps* and a Best Novella award for her short story in the anthology *A Very Special Love*. She lives in central Florida with her family.

TEMPTATION'S
Song

JANICE SIMS

KIMANI

KIMANI PRESS™

Recycling programs for this product may not exist in your area.

ISBN-13: 978-0-373-86170-5

TEMPTATION'S SONG

www.kimanipress.com

Printed in U.S.A.

Dear Reader,

Some friendships last a lifetime. *Temptation's Song* is the first of what I'm calling the Temptation Books, a trio of books about three friends who met at Juilliard, a performing arts school in New York City. In three different disciplines—Elle Jones in voice, Patrice Sutton in theater and Belana Whitaker in classical dance—they were not in direct competition with each other, but they were always there to support and lean on one another through times both good and bad. Be sure to look for *Temptation's Kiss* and *Temptation's Dance* in the coming months.

If you'd like to write to me you can do so at Jani569432@aol.com, or visit my Web site at www.janicesims.com. You can also find me on Facebook, and I have a reading group on Yahoo. If you're not online yet you can write me at P.O. Box 811, Mascotte, FL 34753-0811.

Best always,

Janice Sims

Author's Note

When I was a teenager I saw Grace Bumbry perform in Bizet's *Carmen*. I think it must have been on PBS. I didn't understand a word she sang, but just by the power and beauty of her voice, I was mesmerized. In December 2009 she was one of the recipients of the Kennedy Center Honors. I might not have ever thought to write about an opera singer if I hadn't seen her perform all those many years ago.

Chapter 1

Dominic Corelli sat in a balcony box at Teatro alla Scala, brooding. The room was dark, as he had requested. No one in the theater could see him, but he could hear and, when he stood, see everything going on below.

The opera house in Milan, Italy, had undergone several renovations since its opening in 1778 and today was one of the world's most famous theaters. *Maybe,* Dominic thought, his mind roaming because the singer auditioning for him was performing badly, *the architects were too good.* Thanks to the wonderful acoustics in the auditorium he could hear every off-key note she was warbling.

"Grazie!" he exclaimed, denoting he'd heard enough.

The mezzo-soprano onstage, a petite Italian woman in her midthirties, realizing her time was up, abruptly stopped singing and smiled in the direction of his voice. "*Grazie,* Maestro," she said before exiting the stage.

Because her voice had not been up to par, Dominic didn't rise from his seat to get a glimpse of her. When auditioning singers, he preferred them to sing a cappella, and to be hidden from his view. To him the *voice* was everything. Lately the opera world was becoming as shallow as other forms of theater by showing favoritism to physically attractive performers. He remained true to the art form by hiring gifted singers rather than those who were easy on the eyes but possessed mediocre talent.

True, the role these singers were auditioning for was that of Adama, a woman who was so desirable that she could tempt Satan himself to give up his throne in hell for her. But in the story the devil had first been drawn to her singing, so Dominic was looking for a singer with a truly remarkable voice.

Yet, after three days of auditioning every mezzo-soprano in Europe, it seemed, Dominic hadn't heard that voice.

His cell phone rang. Seeing that the caller was Roberto Ribisi, a La Scala employee who was assisting him during the auditions, he answered, "Roberto?"

"It's nearly lunchtime. Do you want to break now, and continue at one-thirty?"

"How many more have we to go?" Dominic asked.

"Seven," Roberto replied with a tired sigh.

Dominic smiled. He did not envy Roberto the job of keeping a bevy of sopranos happy. Opera singers weren't called divas for nothing. They could be very demanding. Plus, poor Roberto was easily smitten by a pretty face. He imagined the women were trying to twist him around their fingers, hoping for a choice spot in the lineup to go onstage. In actuality, there was no choice spot. Dominic treated them all equally.

He was casting roles for his third opera, *Temptation.* He had worked with several of the women auditioning for the role of Adama. Still, he had no favorites. The moment the woman who deserved the role began to sing for him, he would recognize her.

He didn't care if she was an established singer or a newcomer. All that mattered was that the purity of his composition be maintained. And for that to happen, he needed someone who was fresh, passionate and had the voice of an angel.

"Let's just get this over with," Dominic decided, not believing they would find whom they were looking for today. "Then I can go home and drown my sorrows in a good bottle of Chianti."

"Very well," said Roberto resignedly.

They rang off, and Dominic heard Roberto ask the next singer to take the stage.

Dominic settled back in his chair in the dark to listen. He closed his eyes and said a silent prayer that this would soon be over.

Three singers later, his prayers were answered. He leaned forward, rapt, his heart beating excitedly. Her voice was pure and clean. It was as if he were in the middle of a primeval forest standing beside a waterfall, listening to the crystal-clear water pour forth.

She was singing an aria from one of his earlier operas. He had never heard it sung with such passion before. The tone of her voice as it dipped and soared brought tears to his eyes. He wanted to get up and watch her as she finished the song but forced himself to sit there until her voice trailed off.

Then he rose and went to get a look at her. He couldn't see her clearly because every soprano in the house had run onto the stage to hug her and congratulate her. Those who had merely clapped for the previous singers had to acknowledge that they were in the presence of an exceptional singer.

This went on for several minutes. He had to phone Roberto to ask him to herd the singers off the stage, save for the last performer.

After everyone was seated again, Dominic looked down at the back of a tall, shapely woman wearing jeans, a T-shirt and athletic shoes. Her black, curly hair fell to the middle of her back and she was wearing a tiny backpack purse that Dominic found ridiculous. He laughed to himself. She was dressed like one of those kids who backpack across Europe for the summer as a graduation present to themselves. Still, she was somehow compelling to look at.

She was talking animatedly to Roberto, who was onstage with her. Even from this distance, Dominic could tell Roberto was taken with her.

She hadn't turned around so that he could get a good look at her. *Must I phone him again to get her to turn around?* Dominic thought irritably.

Then he realized that it was he who was being foolish. He had been so mesmerized by her voice that he had forgotten that the next move was his: he could either say thank you and send her on her way, or step up and say, "What's your name?"

He did the latter and she turned around, smiled and said, "Elle, Elle Jones."

Dominic smiled. She was an African-American with flawless reddish-brown skin and huge, dark eyes, so dark they looked black from this distance, a nice contrast to her skin tone. And, he noticed, a full, sensually curved mouth, made for kissing.

She continued to smile up at him and Dominic knew that the role of Adama was hers.

He quickly dialed Roberto's cell phone.

"Yes?" Roberto answered.

"She's the one. But we can't insult the last three ladies by refusing to hear their auditions. Ask Signorina Jones to take a seat and, when we're done with the others, bring her to me."

In all the excitement of auditioning for Dominic Corelli, Elle had forgotten to be nervous. However, when Mr. Corelli's assistant asked her to take a seat in the front row, which every singer knew meant that they were interested in her, she felt her legs go slightly weak.

Trembling inside, she sat down.

She was a bundle of nerves. She was so excited it took every ounce of self-control she had to keep from jumping out of her seat and dancing for joy.

She didn't hear the remaining three singers' auditions. Her head was in the clouds, wondering what it would be like to meet Dominic Corelli. She had been following his career for six years now, ever since his first opera, *Inferno,* had debuted right here at La Scala. With *Inferno* he had joined the ranks of composers like Verdi, Rossini and Puccini, whose careers had all started here. She'd read that back then, not only had those composers written the operas that premiered here at La Scala, they had also conducted the orchestras during the performances. Dominic Corelli directed his operas, although he hired a professional conductor to lead the orchestra during staging of his operas.

Elle was here due to pure luck. She and her friends Belana and Patrice had been treated to a European tour by Belana's father. Milan was a stop they had to make because Belana was not coming to Europe without a visit to the fashion capital, and Elle not without seeing Teatro alla Scala. When they got to Milan, Elle bought a newspaper. She had learned Italian in school. She wanted to brush up on it by reading a daily paper while she was in Italy. That's when she saw the announcement that Dominic Corelli was holding open auditions for his newest opera, *Temptation*. This was unheard of. A composer of his stature usually only auditioned established singers, but an open audition meant that anyone could try out for the part of Adama, the heroine in *Temptation*. Elle could not pass up this opportunity!

She, Belana and Patrice were all graduates of Juilliard, the performing arts school in New York City. She was an opera singer who had understudied several established mezzo-sopranos in major productions and she was a member of the chorus of the Metropolitan Opera. At only twenty-five, she was doing pretty well. However, she wanted the brass ring: a starring role.

She had heard that Dominic Corelli was forward-thinking, a maverick. If he liked her, really liked her, he might take a chance on her and give her the role of Adama.

Even if he didn't give her the role, at least she had fulfilled one of her goals in life: to sing the music of a living composer in his presence. After all, opera houses all over the world today mostly performed works by composers who were long dead.

"Ms. Jones?"

Elle looked up. Roberto was standing in front of her with his hand stretched out toward her. She took it and rose from her seat. The other singers around them were slowly leaving the auditorium.

Roberto, who was five seven to Elle's five nine, leaned toward her. "Mr. Corelli wants to see you in private. Right this way."

"Okay," Elle whispered. Suddenly, her voice was cracking. *Stay calm,* she told herself. *Don't look all bug-eyed with excitement. You'll scare the man!*

Five minutes later she was being led into a private box at the top of the theater. She noticed that the dominant colors at La Scala were red and gold. The chairs and walls were covered with red velvet and the individual opera boxes were painted gold. It was very opulent and very Old World. It was easy to imagine patrons dressed in finery sitting in their private boxes, peering down onto the stage through opera glasses.

She was still admiring her surroundings when Roberto interrupted her thoughts. "Ms. Jones, may I present Dominic Corelli."

Dominic Corelli turned around and Elle forgot to breathe. He had to be the most attractive male she'd ever seen. The son of an African-American opera singer and an Italian clothing manufacturer, he'd inherited the best traits of both races. His skin was a dark golden-brown and he had a day's growth of beard on his square-chinned face. Dark brown, wavy hair was cut close to his scalp and tapered at the back of his neck.

When he smiled at her, dimples appeared in both cheeks and straight white teeth gleamed in his dark face. She was glad Roberto was still holding on to her arm.

"Please leave us, Roberto," he said in lightly accented English.

Elle steeled herself for Roberto to let go of her. She did not swoon, but her legs were definitely giving her signals that she should sit down. In parting, Roberto smiled warmly at her, and that helped somewhat to calm her nerves.

Dominic cleared his throat and gestured to one of the red velvet-upholstered golden chairs. "*Buon giorno.* Shall we sit?"

Elle blinked, took a deep breath and then sat down. Dominic sat, too, and stretched his long legs out in front of him. His gaze swept over her face for a few moments that were nervous on Elle's part. Then he smiled at her. "You have a good voice."

"*Grazie,*" Elle managed, although the volume was little more than a whisper. She was being childish. She took a deep breath, sat up straighter on her chair and looked him squarely in the eyes.

"Where did you study?" he asked, thick brows rising in interest.

"Juilliard," she said confidently. "I graduated nearly four years ago. I was hired by the Metropolitan Opera and have been in the chorus ever since. I've also been the understudy to Denyce Graves, among others."

"How did you like being an understudy?"

"I'm grateful to those who've allowed me to learn from them," Elle said with sincerity. "They were all gracious ladies."

Dominic fell silent for a few moments, as if he were contemplating what she had said. Elle thought she might melt under his intense scrutiny. Those smoldering, dark eyes seemed to expose every one of her vulnerabilities. She felt naked.

Suddenly, he gave her a warm smile. "As I'm sure you will be to your understudy," he said. "You're going to make a wonderful Adama."

He rose and Elle followed suit, unaware of what was proper to do next: shake his hand or hug him? He bent and kissed her on both cheeks. Elle breathed in the male scent of him. He smelled so good, she wanted to lean in and sniff him like a hound dog on a foxhunt. She resisted. Instead, in her excitement, she thanked him profusely: "Oh, God, thank you. All of those more seasoned singers, I didn't think I had a chance! I can never thank you enough for giving me the opportunity."

Dominic felt her body tremble a bit as he let go of her shoulders and peered into her eyes. His lips curved in a smile. He was plainly amused by her outburst. "You may not be thanking me a few weeks from now. I'm told I'm the devil to work for."

Elle grinned up at him. "I'm sure we'll work well together." She had heard rumors that he was a bear to work for, but she chose not to believe them. In the world of opera he was considered a genius. Dominic Corelli's shows sold out in a matter of hours after the tickets went on sale. Also, opera critics, who were notoriously elitist, raved about his productions. If she kept her wits about her and worked hard, this role could make her a star.

Remembering her promise to phone Patrice and Belana as soon as she knew the results of the audition, she pulled off her backpack purse. Looking at Dominic questioningly, she said, "I have people waiting to hear how the audition went. Is it okay with you if I quickly phone them? When do rehearsals start?"

"Of course, and in two weeks," Dominic answered, smiling. He watched as she rummaged in the purse and retrieved a cell phone. "First things first," he added. "I'll need the number of your agent so that a contract can be negotiated."

Elle stared up at him with wide eyes. "My agent?" she croaked.

"You *do* have an agent?"

"No, I negotiated my own contract. I got the maximum for a member of the chorus."

Dominic grimaced. Could she possibly be as naive as she appeared to be? Talented, but entirely too trusting. A less scrupulous person would exploit this opportunity to take advantage of her.

He cleared his throat as he glared down at her. "Then who's been looking out for your best interests?"

Elle blushed. "I have."

Dominic laughed. "Then you have a law degree as well as a degree in—what is it you earned a degree in at Juilliard?"

"Music," Elle said irritably.

"Music," he calmly repeated. "That's such a broad subject."

"Voice," Elle provided, eyes narrowed. "I'm also a classically trained pianist."

To this, Dominic smiled. He liked the idea of his lead soprano also being a classically trained pianist. She may have an ear for composition. He was excited by the possibility that Elle Jones might prove to be stimulating to work with. "Prove it," he challenged.

Elle had the cell phone open and was about to press a button that would connect her with Belana and Patrice, waiting outside in the Piazza del Duomo.

She closed the phone and with her head held high, said, "Lead the way."

Dominic gestured for her to precede him out of the room. Once they were in the hallway, he said, "There's a grand piano downstairs where you auditioned. What will you play for me?"

"One of your compositions," she told him, surprising him. Elle relished the astonished expression on his handsome face.

She didn't tell him that she had been the lead soprano in *Inferno* her senior year at Juilliard and had learned the entire score. That's how she had chosen to sing the aria from *Inferno* for him.

Once they reached the auditorium, Elle sat at the piano and Dominic stood beside it, a smirk on his face—or was that a small smile? Elle couldn't tell. Whatever it was, she intended to wipe it right off his face.

She launched into *Burn in Hell*. Dominic's music was modern opera. It was passionate, inducing all sorts of emotions in the listener. It could be gently stirring or chaotic and jarring. It could be rhythmically moving and actually make listeners want to dance. It could make them laugh or make them cry. In some instances it was downright funky. The one thing it wasn't was forgettable.

Elle recalled every note of *Burn in Hell,* and she played it beautifully. When she finished and slowly raised her hands from the piano keys, there were tears in her eyes. She brushed them away with the pads of her fingers as she smiled up at him.

Dominic shook his head disbelievingly. "*Bellissimo!* How did you remember that piece so well? It's a difficult composition."

Elle laughed shortly. "It's nothing miraculous, really. I learned to play by ear when I was a kid. When I started taking piano lessons, my teacher had a hard time making me learn to read notes. I resisted for a long time. But when I got accepted at Juilliard, I knew I wouldn't be able to fool my instructors there so I buckled down and learned. But I can still play by ear."

Dominic smiled at her. "I like you, Ms. Jones. I like you a lot."

Elle returned his smile. "*Molte grazie,* Maestro."

"But you're going to have to hire an agent. La Scala's lawyers don't negotiate with singers," he said sternly.

Chapter 2

Patrice and Belana were waiting for Elle in front of the Duomo, the third largest church in the world. That morning they had agreed that while Elle was auditioning for Dominic Corelli, Patrice and Belana would be making a circuit through the Quadrilatero della Moda, the fashionable shopping district not far from La Scala and the Duomo.

When Elle spotted them she started screaming, "I got the role! I got the role!"

Both of her friends screamed as well and began running toward her. Other pedestrians on Piazza del Duomo didn't appear startled by their screeching and calmly moved out of the girls' path.

Patrice Sutton, five seven and athletic, reached Elle first and hugged her tightly. "Oh, girl, I'm so happy for you. It's about time you got out of that chorus and got the chance to shine!"

Belana Whitaker, five four and even more athletic than Patrice due to more than twenty years of practicing ballet, hip-bumped Patrice aside for her chance at Elle. Patrice peered down her nose at her shorter friend and let the affront pass. Belana was bossy. Always had been; always would be. Patrice and Elle usually overlooked that particular personality trait of their petite friend, even though it was very irritating.

They jokingly referred to it as Belana's Napoleon complex. Being smaller than either of them, she felt the need to throw her weight around from time to time.

Elle and Belana were jumping up and down with glee. "And you didn't even want to come to Italy!" Belana cried. "We had to twist your arm."

Belana's light brown eyes sparkled with happiness as she looked up at Elle. She let go of Elle and the three of them began walking along the piazza. "Tell us all about it," she ordered.

Elle was distracted by their beautiful surroundings. Didn't they realize they were standing in the midst of history? The Duomo, the cathedral in front of which they stood, had been built in the fourteen hundreds and was a marvel of Gothic architecture. It was so huge it took up an entire side of the piazza. It consisted of several stories of sand-toned stone and its spires reached for the heavens. The day before they had toured the church and it had taken them some time to explore the entire structure.

"Isn't it awe inspiring?" Elle asked no one in particular as she gazed up at it.

Both of her friends sighed impatiently. They didn't want to hear another history lesson. Elle had been filling their heads with background information on every site they had visited since their trip had begun. It wasn't as if they were going to remember any of it once they were back in New York City. Patrice and Belana were more interested in mingling with the natives, especially the male natives.

"You were going to tell us about the audition, not more about architecture," Belana reminded Elle. "I already know more about Gothic buildings than I ever wanted to know."

"I know *that's* right!" Patrice agreed.

They sandwiched Elle between them as they headed in the direction of the Galleria Vittorio Emanuele II, where they would find a café and have lunch.

Both girls carried shopping bags and were casually dressed, as Elle was: Belana in a red T-shirt and white city shorts with sandals, and Patrice in jeans, a short-sleeved white blouse and Crocs. Belana had golden-brown skin and naturally wavy auburn hair that she wore long so that when she was dancing in a ballet she could put it up in the customary French knot at the back of her neck. Patrice had rich medium-brown skin and jet-black hair that she wore relaxed, short and layered. She liked what she called wash-and-wear hair, because as an actress her looks were always being altered for a role. She spent enough time in the makeup chair on the set of the sitcom where she was lucky enough to be a regular. Of the three of them, she was the most successful. She had also recently played significant parts in two films that had received excellent reviews when they had debuted at theaters.

Elle was the only child of a single mother who had raised her in Harlem. Patrice was the second child in a four-sibling family. She was raised by both parents on a ranch in New Mexico. Belana was the spoiled daughter of one of the richest men in America. She had an older brother and her family owned homes in six locations around the world. Her parents had been divorced since she was a toddler and her father had won custody of her and her brother. She hadn't seen her mother in years.

Since their meeting at Juilliard six years ago they had supported each other through broken hearts, botched auditions and anything else life threw at them.

They found a small café and sat down at a sidewalk table.

A waiter appeared and offered them menus. Elle waved them off. "We'd like today's special," she told him in Italian, "and a bottle of your house wine."

When the waiter had gone, Belana complained, "You know I hate it when you do that, Patty, and I don't know what you're saying. You could be ordering us squid or something equally horrible."

Elle laughed shortly. "If you hear the word *calamari,* head for the hills."

"Calamari," Belana repeated, as if trying to commit the word to memory.

"Stop stalling," Patrice told Elle. "Tell us about Dominic Corelli. Do his photos do him justice?"

"Not even close," Elle admitted, her gaze flitting from Patrice's face to Belana's. Both women leaned toward her so that they wouldn't miss a word she was about to say. "First of all, he's taller than I imagined he would be. How many tall men have you seen since we've been in Italy?"

"They're not *that* short," Belana said in defense of Italian men. "Several have been taller than I am."

"You're only five four," said Patrice. "Anyway," she

added, turning her attention back to Elle, "he has an African-American mother, doesn't he? He probably got his height from her side of the family. What happened after your audition?"

"He told me he thought I was talented, and then he laughed at me when I told him I didn't have an agent. He treated me like a not-so-bright child. I felt like an amateur telling him I negotiated my own contracts."

"I've been telling you for years that you need an agent," Belana said. She went into her purse and withdrew her BlackBerry. "I'm sending Fred a message. He can represent you."

Patrice sniffed derisively. "Fred? He's a pussycat compared to my agent, Blanca. This is Elle's big chance. She needs Blanca."

"Blanca Mendes is a shark in designer shoes," Belana accused.

"Yeah, she wears nice things because her clients always get good deals. Face it, Belana. If you weren't already rich, you would want her to represent you, too. It just so happens that you're a dancer because you love it, not because it's your way of putting food on the table."

"I'm a good dancer!" Belana cried, hurt.

"You're the best dancer in your company," Patrice readily admitted. "That's why it pains me that you're not earning what you're worth!"

Patrice was always interested in the bottom line. She had seen her parents struggling to keep the ranch going over the years. As one of four siblings, she had known what it felt like to wear discount-store clothes to school and have some of the more obnoxious kids look down on her. That's why she worked so hard and why she had hired an agent who was a shark.

Belana sighed loudly and regarded Elle with a smile. "She's right. Hire the shark."

"What if she won't represent me?" Elle asked innocently.

Belana and Patrice looked at each other and burst out laughing.

"Just mention Dominic Corelli's name, stand back and watch the shark attack," said Patrice.

The waiter brought their wine and served them.

Belana, who was more wine savvy than her friends, took a sip first and declared, "Not bad!"

The waiter smiled. "I'm glad you like it."

"You speak English!" Elle cried, grinning.

"Of course," he said with a naughty wink in Elle's direction. He placed the wine bottle on the table. "I will return shortly with your fresh trout served with risotto and vegetables. My name is Paolo."

"Thank you, Paolo," Elle said.

He smiled at her again and left.

Belana shook her head in admiration and said, "He's not too short for me!"

"But he *is* too young," Patrice said. "He can't be more than eighteen."

"Isn't that considered an adult in Italy?" asked Belana.

Belana and Patrice looked to Elle for the answer.

Elle hunched her shoulders. "I don't know!" To which Patrice and Belana laughed.

"Finally," said Belana. "A subject Elle knows nothing about."

"Honestly, can we stay on the subject here?" Patrice

complained, turning to Elle. "You said he was taller than you thought he would be. What else? You can't have been in the room with a man that talented and good-looking without forming an opinion of him."

Elle was remembering the sensuality with which Dominic Corelli moved. How his body, underneath his suit, had seemed so powerful. Warmth suffused her. "He's the sexiest man I've ever met," she emphatically stated. "I'm glad he's going to be my boss because if he were just another unattached singer in the production, I would probably be tempted to date him."

"Tempted to date him?" Patrice mimicked in a prim and proper tone. It was her opinion that Elle was too guarded with her emotions since she'd been dumped by her last boyfriend. She practiced her craft endlessly, professing to her friends that when her big break presented itself, she was damned well going to be ready for it. As a result of her dedication, she had no love life to speak of. "You don't date a sexy beast, girl, you jump his bones!"

"Throw him down and have your way with him," Belana offered, getting into the ribbing of Elle.

"Turn him on, rip his clothes off and see if he'll salute," said Patrice.

"And if he salutes, see if he can go the distance," added Belana.

Elle laughed. "Keep dreaming, guys. You know I could never come on to a man like Dominic Corelli."

"What if he comes on to *you?*" Patrice asked.

Elle was stumped. Excited by the prospect, but definitely without a notion of what she would do if Dominic Corelli actually admitted he wanted to sleep with her.

"Let me enjoy the fact that he wants me in his opera," she told them. "The idea of his wanting me in his bed is beyond me." She laughed. "Besides, believe me, he doesn't see me as a potential sexual conquest. He's already laughed at my ignorance and told me he's the devil to work for. So, don't go dreaming up sexy scenarios in your love-starved minds!"

"Love-starved," said Belana, offended. "I'm dating *two* men. And Patty is fighting off the advances of every horny actor in Hollywood."

Patrice laughed. "You're exaggerating a bit, my dear. I really *am* love-starved. I haven't been on a date in five months. You're representing all of us when it comes to dating."

Belana snapped her fingers at them. "I've got it like that!"

Elle and Patrice laughed at her. "She's not at all humble about it," observed Elle.

At that instant, Paolo arrived with a food-laden tray and served their meals with a flourish. "Enjoy!"

They did. Seasoned with savory spices, the trout was baked to perfection and the risotto, made with saffron, was a delicate, appropriate accompaniment to the fish.

When they were finished they called Paolo over, gave him a nice gratuity, for which he thanked them, and sent their compliments to the chef. Paolo waved to them as they walked away.

When they were nearly out of earshot he grinned and exclaimed, *"Bella!"*

Chapter 3

The next day, Dominic was in the office of his spacious apartment in Milan watching the performances of the previous day's singers on a flat-screen TV. He wanted to make sure that choosing Elle Jones for the female lead had been the right decision. Maybe he had imagined the tone of her voice? After all, by the time she came along he was so tired of auditioning singers that he'd begun to pray to be delivered from the task. He could have latched onto any competent singer.

A competent singer wasn't all he needed for this role. He needed a star, someone the audience would be instantly enamored with and continue to love from opening night to closing night.

When he got to Elle Jones's performance and saw her walk onto the stage, he felt his stomach muscles painfully constrict. It was a reaction he'd stopped having at the sight of a beautiful woman when he was in his teens. The feeling was a mixture of anticipation and excitement with a bit of sexual desire thrown in.

He was glad he had not been watching her yesterday when she had sung for him. He would have had this same reaction before she had even opened her mouth, and who knew? His decision to hire her could have been based on sexual desire.

He was only human.

On the screen, she began to sing, and the expression on her face was sublime. It was obvious she loved the song and it was also clear that she wasn't performing for him, but was singing to heaven. His mother had told him that her own best performances were not sung for an audience in an opera house, but a heavenly audience: God and his angels. She imagined that she was entertaining angels and it gave a certain quality to her voice that she was never able to duplicate when she wasn't in that mind-set during a performance.

It was a feeling, according to his mother, that was hard to explain. But she said she had felt closer to heaven during those times than she had ever felt while sitting in a church.

Dominic believed her because when he was creating music he also felt more connected with God, the universe or whatever a person thought of as a higher power.

Could Elle Jones be a believer?

He smiled the entire time she was singing, and then he used the remote to stop the DVD player. Yes, Elle Jones had been the right choice, but there was something about her that made him wary. She was so young, only twenty-five, and inexperienced. Plus, there was the fact that he was wildly attracted to her. That could pose a problem. He made it a rule to never get personally involved with colleagues or staff. It could get messy. Artists were notoriously emotional creatures. His own personality could get volatile at times, especially when he was trying to bring his work to life on the stage. Would he be able to work with Elle Jones every day without growing evermore attracted to her? Also, the fact that she was attracted to him hadn't escaped his notice. She had trembled at his touch, after all. Was she worth the effort?

He watched her performance one more time.

Yes, she was.

A couple of nights later, an unsuspecting Dominic got another dose of Elle Jones.

It was Saturday night and he was out on the town with his cousin, Gianni Romano. Gianni was the only son of his *tia* Maria, his father's youngest sister. Of his father's three sisters, Tia Maria had been the only one who hadn't turned a cold shoulder to his new African-American bride when he'd brought her home to meet the family. Subsequently Tia Maria and Dominic's mother, Natalie, had become best friends. The other sisters had come around eventually, but by then Dominic and Gianni had already forged a strong bond, as he and his mother spent a lot of time visiting Tia Maria. The women had encouraged the first cousins' friendship because they wanted them to be close. Later, Tia Maria would give birth to a daughter, Dona Maria, and Natalie would give birth to two daughters, Ana and Sophia.

He and Gianni, who worked in the fashion industry alongside Dominic's father, Carlo, had dined and were talking about their family when Dominic's cell phone rang.

Gianni had been in the middle of telling him about his toddler's new skill at launching himself like a daredevil off furniture, the greater the height the better. Dominic gazed down at the number on his cell phone's display, saw that it was the police and quickly answered.

An officer said that they had a young American woman in custody and she had given them his number as someone who could vouch for her.

"What is the young woman's name?" Dominic asked.

"Elle Jones," said the officer.

"Exactly what is she charged with?" Dominic asked, astonished.

"Striking a police officer," was the answer.

Before hanging up, Dominic asked for the address of the police station, assured the officer he did know Elle Jones and that he would be there as soon as possible.

Regarding Gianni across the table, he frowned. "Elle Jones is in jail for hitting a cop." Dominic had told him all about Elle over dinner

Gianni laughed. "I like her already."

"I'd better get over there before she takes the entire police station hostage," joked Dominic, shaking his head.

The cousins rose and Dominic placed enough money on the table to cover their bill plus a generous tip. "Tell Francesca hello for me and buy little Gianni a helmet. He'll soon graduate to trying to jump off the roof."

"God forbid," said Gianni. "Let me know how Signorina Jones fares."

In front of the restaurant Gianni went to his Jaguar and Dominic to his Range Rover, where he sat behind the wheel for a moment, wondering why Elle Jones had struck a cop.

He started the car. He would soon find out.

Elle sat in the communal room of the police station alongside muggers, prostitutes and she didn't know how many more types of criminals. She, Belana and Patrice had gone to dinner earlier in the evening and then she had gone to the train station to see them off to Rome. She was remaining in Milan in order to find an apartment and finish her paperwork. Her new agent had told her she needed to fill out the forms before she would be allowed to live and work in Italy during the time it would take to rehearse and star in Dominic Corelli's new opera.

As she had been walking back from the train station, which was not far from her hotel, she was accosted by a strange man. He had apparently found her irresistible in her evening attire, a modest, sleeveless white dress, its hem falling about two inches above her knees, and a pair of white, strappy sandals. Without saying a word, and for no conceivable reason, he had reached out and pinched her on the behind as she had passed him. Right after that, Elle had turned around and slapped him across the face as hard as she could.

It hadn't ended there, though. He had obviously taken her slap as an invitation, because he'd grabbed her and pulled her roughly against his chest. Even though they were about the same height, he was very strong and Elle couldn't push out of his embrace.

She'd struggled, desperately looking around for

someone to come to her aid. But the people passing them on the street had looked away, not wanting to get involved.

"Let go of me!" she'd yelled at him.

"Isn't this what you tourists want when you come to Italia?" he'd asked, leering at her.

His breath had reeked of stale wine. Elle had tried to push him away, jerking her head back from him as he tried to kiss her. She felt something hard on his left side under his jacket. He was carrying a gun.

Now she panicked. Was she going to be attacked and killed on a Milan street?

Well, if he was going to try to harm her, she'd just as well go for broke. She kneed him. She heard the breath escape his throat and smelled his vile exhalation. Then she ran for her life, right into the arms of a uniformed police officer.

She was never happier to see anyone in her life. "Officer!" she cried in Italian, pointing at the man, who was doubled over in pain. "That man grabbed me against my will. And he has a gun!"

To her horror the man she had kneed removed a policeman's badge from his inside jacket pocket and wheezed, "She's under arrest for attacking an officer."

"Me?" Elle cried, indignant. "He attacked *me!* Smell his breath—he's drunk—drunk and out accosting innocent tourists. He told me I was asking for it!"

The uniformed policeman calmly cuffed her. "Miss, I advise you not to say anything else until you call your lawyer."

So that's how she had come to be handcuffed to a chair, sitting beside a bottle blonde who was dressed in a black leather dominatrix outfit and matching thigh-high boots. The woman smiled at her. "New to this part of town?" she asked in Italian.

She obviously thought Elle was a working girl, too.

"Very new," Elle replied.

"I thought so," said the woman, her black eyes roaming over Elle's clothes. "You're wearing white. There isn't much demand for innocence anymore. They can find that on the Internet these days." She reached inside her cleavage and produced a business card. "But you have potential. I'm Violetta. Call me and I'll get you on the right track."

Elle accepted the card and put it in her own cleavage. "Thanks."

Violetta smiled. "We girls have to look out for one another." She sneered at an officer who passed too close to their chairs. "Why are you people so slow?" she hissed at him. "Some of us have better places to be. Move your asses!"

The police officer bowed in her direction. "So sorry to keep you waiting, madam," he said sarcastically.

Violetta kicked at him with her stiletto-heeled boot. He quickly jumped out of range.

"That's right, run, you coward!" She laughed with satisfaction.

Elle glanced down at her watch. They had confiscated her purse, but let her keep her watch. It was after eleven. She wondered if they had actually phoned Dominic Corelli or had simply told her they would.

They had laughed at her when she had told them she had been hired by Dominic Corelli to appear in his next opera. She imagined that he was well-known here in Milan, and well respected. The derisive looks she'd gotten after making her claim was proof of that. They thought she was a raving lunatic.

She had hated to have to contact him, but she didn't know anyone else in Milan. After this, he would probably inform her that he no longer wanted her in his opera. Hell, he probably wouldn't even want her in his city.

Frowning, she sat up straighter on her chair and held her head up high. Why was she being pessimistic? She hadn't done anything wrong. That drunken cop had put his filthy hands on her and if she hadn't defended herself he might have done much more.

But how would she prove her innocence?

"Elle?"

Elle looked up into Dominic's face. He smiled. She grimaced. "Signor Corelli, I'm innocent, I swear."

"I know you are," he said comfortingly.

He gestured to an officer standing nearby, who stepped forward and unlocked Elle's handcuffs.

Elle looked on in amazement. Was that all it had taken, for Dominic Corelli to show up and vouch for her? If so, this was a crazy country. What about her rights as a human being? What about being innocent until proven guilty?

She stared up at him as she got to her feet. "What's going on? Did they catch that officer in a lie?"

A short, middle-aged man in a dark gray suit came up behind Dominic and tapped him on the shoulder. Dominic turned around.

"You can take Signorina Jones home," said the man. "The off-duty officer who accused her of striking him admitted that he had too much to drink tonight and may have behaved inappropriately toward Signorina Jones when he met her on the street."

"Thank you," Dominic said, shaking the gentleman's hand. "I apologize for waking you, Felix, but Signorina Jones needed someone who knows his way around the legal system."

"That's why your family has me on retainer," the lawyer said pleasantly. He smiled at Elle. "I'm so sorry you had to go through that very uncomfortable experience, Signorina."

"Thank you," Elle said in a low voice. She was so relieved that she felt tears fill her eyes. She didn't allow them to fall, though.

"You can pick up your belongings on the way out and all evidence of this incident will be struck from the record. Except, of course, your statement about the condition the officer was in when he accosted you. That will remain on his record. He is being severely disciplined for his behavior."

Elle felt some satisfaction upon hearing this news, and even though she wanted to press charges and see him punished to the full extent of the law, she wanted to get out of there even more.

"Thank you so much," she said again to the lawyer.

Felix left and Dominic offered Elle his arm. She took it, grateful for his support. He led her over to the evidence room, where she retrieved her purse, made sure everything was in it and they left the police station arm in arm.

Outside, Elle breathed in the night air and looked up at the black sky. The city sparkled around them. Traffic, lighter at night but still somewhat heavy, made a racket as late-night pedestrians strolled leisurely down the streets.

"Are you all right?" Dominic asked quietly.

Elle met his eyes and smiled wanly. "Not really. But I will be after a good night's sleep. I can't let that guy freak me out. I've got an opera to star in, if you still want me, and nothing and no one is going to get in the way of that."

Dominic laughed softly as he led her to his car. "Of course I still want you. Do you think I would get on the wrong side of a woman with your punching power? I saw that cop's face. It's already turning purple!"

Elle laughed. "He had it coming."

Dominic knew those were just brave words. Elle was still upset. He felt her body shake with nerves as he helped her into the car.

Once inside Elle tried to relax against the leather seat. Dominic started the car and pulled into traffic. "Where are you staying?"

She told him. He was glad she was staying at a nice hotel with twenty-four-hour security. He would feel better about leaving her alone tonight. At least, that's what he told himself as he drove the few blocks to the hotel. By the time he had parked in their lot, he had made up his mind that he wasn't going to leave her alone tonight under any circumstances, and he didn't care how much she protested.

They sat in the car a few moments after he'd turned off the engine. He turned to her. "Look, Elle, you've had a shock to the system, and I don't think you should stay by yourself tonight."

She started to protest but he stopped her. "If you

won't let me in the room, I'll sleep outside your door. But I'm not leaving you alone tonight."

They gazed into each other's eyes. Elle could tell he was determined. "There are two bedrooms in the suite. You can have one of them," she said, her voice soft.

Dominic breathed a sigh of relief. There was something so vulnerable about Elle. His first instinct was to protect her. Surely he could smother his powerful attraction to her for one night?

Eyes still boring into hers, he said, "Thank you for not fighting me on this."

"I would fight you if I thought you were wrong," Elle assured him. "But the fact is, I just put my friends on the train earlier this evening. I would welcome someone to talk to tonight."

He gave her a grateful smile, which sent her stomach into somersaults. "Then I'm your man."

They got out of the car and went into the hotel.

Chapter 4

"The Met must pay you well," Dominic remarked upon entering the suite. "This is very nice."

Elle locked the door behind them. "I can't afford this. My friend Belana's father, who's a very successful businessman, paid for our trip."

The suite, decorated in modern Italian, had a color scheme of earth tones. The thick carpeting muted their footsteps as they crossed the room. Elle gestured to the pale golden sofa in the living room of the suite. "Have a seat."

Looking back at him over her shoulder, she added, "I'm going to change. These shoes are killing me. There's a bathrobe behind the bathroom door in the spare bedroom, if you'd like to get out of your clothes, too."

Dominic knew this was an innocent suggestion. She just wanted him to be comfortable, but the thought of getting undressed while he was alone with her in a hotel room made him imagine other reasons why she'd ask him to get out of his clothes.

Watching her leave the room, her full, shapely hips moving enticingly beneath the white sheath she had on, he felt his groin tighten. He managed a strangled, "I'm fine, thank you. But you feel free to do whatever it is you do to prepare for bed."

"All right, then. If you say so," she said lightly as she disappeared around the corner, into the hallway.

In her absence, Dominic removed his jacket, loosened his tie, unbuttoned his long-sleeved shirt at the wrists and rolled the cuffs up to his elbows. That was as comfortable as he intended to get tonight.

In her bedroom, Elle hurried to the closet, removed her dress and hung it on a hanger, kicked off her sandals, bent down, picked them up, returned them to their shoe box and placed the box on the closet shelf. Even with Dominic Corelli waiting for her in the next room, she was, admittedly, anal-retentive and couldn't just toss her clothing in the closet.

She went into the adjacent bathroom, ran a brush through her long, curly hair and tied it back with a blue ribbon, washed the makeup off her face and flossed and brushed her teeth. When she stripped to put on her pajamas, Violetta's card fell to the floor. She picked it up. She would keep it as a memento.

Barefooted, she went back into the living room.

Dominic looked up and burst into laughter. "You look like a little girl!"

He had expected her to change into something feminine and soft. He had been hoping for it. Just because he intended not to touch her didn't mean he couldn't get his fill of admiring her.

Elle folded her legs under her as she sat down. Amusement lit up her dark brown eyes. "I'm glad you find my pajamas so funny. That's just the reaction from the opposite sex I was hoping for when I bought them. That, or an irresistible urge to revert to childhood and sit in front of the TV with a big bowl of popcorn and watch cartoons."

His laughter under control, Dominic regarded her with a warm smile. She was an unusual woman, sitting in front of him with her legs tucked beneath her. Her face scrubbed clean of makeup and in pajamas. Either she was the most unsophisticated woman he had ever met, or she was confident about her sexuality.

Admittedly, she looked beautiful without makeup. Her skin was smooth and clear, a lovely shade of brown with red undertones. He bet he could actually detect it when she blushed.

Maybe he should test it.

"Believe me," he said softly, his eyes caressing her face, "I am well aware that you are a fully grown woman underneath those pajamas."

He had been right. She blushed all the way to the tips of her pretty ears. He got a certain satisfaction out of knowing he'd caused that reaction.

Elle cleared her throat. She had to mentally shake herself before she found she could think straight again after that hot flash he'd purposely inflicted on her. She would have to be on guard around him. It was obvious he liked to flirt. She wasn't exactly an amateur herself. But now definitely wasn't the time to practice.

That's why she had put on the armor the pajamas

were meant to be. She hadn't met a man yet who had found them sexy. Except the men who were determined to get her into bed, no matter what. Dominic Corelli couldn't be that hard up for a woman. He could have any woman he wanted. What would he want with a young, inexperienced, albeit *good,* opera singer dying for her big break?

If he were a less scrupulous man he might be coming on to her right now. But she sensed he was an honorable man. Otherwise, she wouldn't have allowed him inside of her hotel room, no matter what he'd said. She was raised in Harlem, after all. She might be young, but she wasn't naive.

Refusing to rise to the bait, she smiled at him and said, "Thank you for tonight. I don't know what I would have done if you hadn't shown up."

Dominic relaxed with his arm along the back of the sofa and stretched out his legs. "I could never have ignored your call," he told her. "You're alone in a strange city. I know it must have been an ordeal for you."

"I thought it was a myth," Elle told him.

"What?"

"That Italian men pinch women tourists on the behind," she said, looking at him with wide eyes. "Patrice, Belana and I went all over Italy and no one touched us inappropriately. I mean, there was flirting going on, on both sides, but no touching! And then along comes that cop, who acted like he took me for a common prostitute. He said that's what women tourists are looking for when they come to Italy." She hugged herself as if she were suddenly chilled to the bone.

"I assure you, most Italian men are respectful of

all women, tourists or otherwise," Dominic said. He wanted to go to her and wrap her in his arms, but thought better of it.

"They are—*we* are—good husbands and fathers. We love our families. You had the bad luck of running into a drunk and a lout. Policemen aren't exempt from foolish behavior. Isn't it true that you can find disrespectful men anywhere on the planet, not just Italy?"

"I know," Elle said, trying to be fair. "I won't let this experience change my opinion of Italy. I've loved my visit here."

Dominic smiled indulgently. "I'm glad."

"Thanks again, Signor Corelli."

Dominic was taken aback when she called him Signor Corelli. But then he remembered that was how she'd addressed him at the police station. She considered him her employer, after all. They hadn't gotten to know each other on a social level yet. Earlier, he had been presumptuous to address her as Elle. But then, he had been a bit emotional upon seeing her sitting next to an apparent prostitute. He'd forgotten social niceties.

"Why don't you call me Dominic?" he said.

Elle blushed again and said, "Maybe when I get to know you better."

Dominic laughed softly and shifted his big body into a more comfortable position on the sofa. "Come now, we're going to be working together. Everyone calls me Dominic."

"I can't," she insisted. "I've spent the last six years studying your work. I think you're a genius and I'm going to have to work my way up to calling you by your first name. So don't insist, because it won't make the process go any faster."

"My father is Signor Corelli," Dominic said. "You make me feel old before my time."

Elle laughed softly. "I know how old you are. You're thirty-three. You're a *young* genius."

"You've done your homework," Dominic said, impressed, "though I'm hardly a genius. What else did you dig up on the Web about me?"

"I didn't have to use the Web to find information on you," she said, smiling secretively.

"Everything I needed was at the public library. Although I did search for you on Google once and there were a lot of hits. But I don't really trust the Web when it comes to accurate information. There's a lot of gossip on it."

Dominic knew this to be true. He had been linked with women on the Web whom he had never met. He was currently supposedly dating Italian actress Mia Serrano. She had come to a couple of his operas at La Scala and been invited backstage, but he had never dated her.

"It's no wonder you were a musical prodigy," Elle continued. "Your mother is one of the greatest mezzo-sopranos of all time, and your grandmother, Renata Corelli, one of Italy's premier sopranos."

Dominic smiled at the mention of his mother and grandmother, both of whom he loved dearly. His grandmother had passed away four years ago. She had doted on him, and he had doted on her. He had been with her when she died, at her favorite place on earth, her villa on Lake Como. He had held her hand as she lay on a chaise longue in the middle of her beloved garden. When she slipped away, there had been a smile on her face as if she were seeing something beautiful in her mind's eye at the moment she succumbed. He had bent and kissed her forehead and whispered, "Rest until we meet again, my darling."

"Yes," he said to Elle. "They were a great influence on me. Among my earliest memories is sitting in the family's box at La Scala watching my grandmother or my mother sing." He looked her straight in the eye. "They were both good in their time. However, they didn't have your talent."

He didn't know why he'd said that. It was true. But he knew, as a director, that it wasn't good to build up a singer's ego too much. Some singers could become impossibly demanding when they knew how you truly felt about their talent.

So he was surprised by Elle's reaction to the compliment. Instead of beaming in satisfaction, she started weeping. It was the most amazing thing to watch. Silent tears fell down her cheeks and her chest began heaving, then all of a sudden the sound came on and she was bawling.

Dominic went to stand up, and Elle held up the palm of her hand, signaling that she wanted him to stay where he was. "Please don't get up," she said through her tears. "I'm just a bit emotional. I mean, since I was a kid people have told me I have a gift but I usually took it for granted. After all, they were my friends and family—they were obligated to encourage me. But for you to tell me you think I'm gifted means everything to me. You can't imagine how much."

When she felt confident enough to meet his gaze, he saw only humility in her eyes and it touched him in ways he'd never felt before.

A crack developed in the mental barriers he'd erected

around his heart, built to guard against feeling too much for a woman lest she begin to mean so much to him that he put her before his work. *It's just a crack,* he told himself. *After tonight, I won't let myself be alone with her. She's some kind of witch. She's made me want her inside of three days.*

Elle got up. "Excuse me," she said, and left the room.

He was glad to see her go. He needed time alone to think.

Five minutes later, his treacherous heart beat excitedly at the sight of her when she returned. He noticed she'd washed her face and had adopted a new attitude.

"Enough about my wonderful talent," she joked. "I know all about your background but you don't know much about mine. Aren't you a little wary about hiring an unknown? What will the Milano opera community have to say about that?"

Dominic felt more at ease with this question. Now he was in his element. "I don't give a damn what they think," he said. He was a bit of an egomaniac and he knew it. Anyone who worked with him knew he was single-minded and didn't allow anyone to dictate how his operas should be cast.

"I have the final say," he told her. "It's in my contract. My work, after all, is my own vision. I know how I want it staged and I know whom I want to portray the characters I created."

Elle grinned and leaned forward. "Who will portray Cristiano, then?"

Cristiano was the name that Satan took in the story line when he was in the guise of a human. In the libretto, he takes great pleasure in using a name so close to that of Christ, the son of God, his greatest nemesis.

Interested in her opinion, Dominic asked, "Who do *you* think would make a good Cristiano?"

"Are we in fantasyland here?" Elle asked. "Or do you want a living singer who can actually play the role? If I could choose anyone from any time, I would say Luciano Pavarotti, in his prime, would have been the perfect Cristiano."

Dominic had to agree. She was very astute, this girl from Harlem. He had imagined Pavarotti when he was composing the music for the opera. "You're right," he told her. "But, sadly, Luciano is no longer with us. Name someone who is still on this plane of existence."

Elle thought for a few minutes and said, "When it comes to the voice you would need and the physical bearing, the ability to project and make a character come alive, it would have to be Spanish tenor Jaime Montoya."

"Montoya," Dominic said, considering the brash young singer. Jaime had a reputation for being arrogant, hard to work with and a womanizer, to boot. Okay, Dominic would be a hypocrite if he held being a womanizer against the singer. He had his fair share of women's names in his little black book, too.

He couldn't deny that Elle had a point. Jaime had the voice and the bearing. He also had a huge following in Europe and elsewhere in the world. As much as Dominic wanted to think that opera aficionados came to his shows simply to enjoy his work, having a box-office draw like Jaime in the role of Cristiano couldn't hurt.

He was auditioning singers for the role next week.

"Elle," he said, looking at her expectantly. "May I call you Elle?"

"Of course, Signor Corelli," said Elle to his utter frustration.

"Would you like to sit in on the auditions for male lead next week? You can join me in my box." The request was impulsive. He'd never asked anyone to sit in before.

"Will Jaime be auditioning?" she asked with a mischievous spark in her eyes.

"Yes, I'm told he'll be there," said Dominic, wondering why she was so interested in the Spanish singer. Did she have a crush on him, or was she only interested in playing opposite him in the opera?

He would not have them carrying on an affair right under his nose!

Taking a deep breath, he mentally checked himself. Why was he getting irritated—and a little jealous, he was man enough to admit—over a scenario that might never unfold, especially if he didn't hire Jaime Montoya?

"I'd love to," Elle said, giving him a gorgeous smile.

His groin grew tight again, and he quickly changed the subject. "All right, that's settled," he said. "Let's talk about practical matters, shall we? Such as where you're going to live while you're here in Milan. My sister, Ana, has an apartment she's going to have to sublet because she's moving to New York. She's a model and has been hired by an agency there. We hate to see her go, but she has to be independent."

He sounded genuinely regretful about his sister moving away. Elle thought he must be very close to Ana

and the note of sadness in his voice made her want to
offer comfort.

"Is she very young?" she asked sympathetically.

"Only twenty-three, a baby," he said. He met her
eyes. "Not much younger than you are. Have you got a
brother who's missing you?"

"I'm afraid not. I wish I did have a brother or a sister,
but after my mom had me when she was eighteen, she
felt I was enough."

"She raised you alone?" asked Dominic. His dark
eyes were full of sympathy.

"Yes, and don't feel sorry for me," said Elle. "I had
a great childhood. Isobel—that's my mother—and I
grew up together and we're very close. Sometimes it felt
more like we were sisters than mother and daughter. We
lived with my grandparents in a brownstone in Harlem.
It has been in the family for more than a hundred years,
according to my grandfather. I know that's not old
compared to your standards, but for America, especially
black America, it's a big thing to say a house has been
in the family for that long. Anyway, something on that
house was always being repaired, but I loved it. Still do.
My grandparents are gone now, but Isobel and I live in
it together. Since I'm working in New York I figured,
why pay rent somewhere else?"

Dominic was smiling at her and he suddenly realized
that he was happy. He would be content to sit up all
night talking to her, but he could tell by the drowsy
expression in her sultry eyes that she was exhausted.
She had had a shock and she needed to rest.

"That's interesting," he said, noting how comforting
it was for her to still be living in her childhood home.
"What comforts you at bedtime nowadays? Should I

read you a story? In your pajamas you look like you might appreciate that approach."

Elle smiled at his humor and yawned daintily with her hand over her mouth before replying, "Sing me an Italian lullaby."

Dominic smiled. She didn't know how adorable she looked curled up in that chair, or how the sound of her voice caused a physical reaction in him. Just sitting across from her for the past half hour had rendered him hard.

"I don't sing," he lied.

"Come now, Signor Corelli," she said softly, her voice a gentle caress. "When you were growing up you took voice lessons."

"You and your research," Dominic said with a short laugh. "If I had been any good at singing, I'd still be doing it. You're the singer. Sing *me* a lullaby."

"Oh, all right," Elle said, pretending to be put-upon. She'd been slouching, so she sat up straight before beginning Keb' Mo's "Lullaby Baby Blues."

"Lullaby baby blues. Time to kick off your walking shoes."

She didn't sound anything like a classically trained singer, many of whom, even when they were singing the blues, made the song sound like classical music. She sounded like a soul singer, her deep voice gritty and very sexy.

When she finished, Dominic wanted to go to her, pull her into his arms and kiss her until both of them were breathless with desire.

Instead he smiled at her and said, "Why do you sing opera when you can do that? There is undoubtedly more money in being a pop star than an opera star."

Returning his smile, Elle answered, "Because even though I like other kinds of music, it's opera I'm passionate about. When I'm on that stage, it's as if I'm transported to a spiritual place. It's as if I'm…"

"Singing to God?" Dominic asked with an expectant expression.

Elle laughed shortly. "Yes, that's it! It's very addictive, that feeling. It feels better than sex!"

"Really?" Dominic said with a smile. If singing was better than sex to her, exactly whom had she been making love to? It had to be someone really inept in bed.

If he ever made love to her she would definitely not compare singing to lovemaking. There would be no comparison.

Elle hid her face, which had grown hot with embarrassment, behind her hands. "I can't believe I said that." She regarded him with laughing eyes. "I think I'll go to bed on that note." She got up. "The bed's already turned down in the spare room. I hope you sleep well. Good night."

Dominic got up, took her hand in his and brought it to his lips. After kissing it, he said with a smile, "*Buona notte,* nightingale. Thank you for that beautiful lullaby."

He released her hand and Elle, blushing, turned and walked away, holding the hand he'd kissed close to her chest. She knew, in spite of the awful incident earlier in the evening, that she would have sweet dreams tonight.

Dominic watched her go. He would definitely burn in his bed tonight, with her only a few feet down the hall from him.

What he needed was a stiff drink, or a cold shower.

He went over to the bar. No liquor. Not even a bottle of wine.

He headed to the spare bedroom. A cold shower was in order. Looked like he'd be using that robe she'd offered him, after all.

Chapter 5

·

The next morning, Elle awakened at half past eight. She showered and then dressed with care, even though she figured that when she walked into the living room of the suite there would be no sign of Dominic Corelli. Having seen her safely through the night, undoubtedly he had fled at the first glimmer of daylight.

She couldn't blame him. Why had she let it slip that she loved singing as much as, maybe more than, sex? Because of that he probably now thought that she was an unsophisticated rube who shouldn't be let loose on the unsuspecting citizens of Milan. She needed to be babysat for her own good, much like a small child needed to be kept away from fire to prevent her from burning herself.

"Buon giorno!"

Dominic Corelli was sitting on the sofa, reading the morning paper, a steaming cup of coffee on the table in front of him. He had put back on his jacket and shoes and straightened his tie. As handsome as ever, he appeared fresh and ready for a business meeting or morning mass.

"Buon giorno," Elle said, smiling warily.

Dominic cast an appreciative eye over her. She was wearing a navy blue wrap dress that accentuated her curves. It wasn't too clingy, with barely a glimpse of cleavage. She wore three-inch-heel pumps in the same shade. Because his family on his father's side had been in the clothing business for many years, he was of the opinion that a woman's clothing should complement her natural beauty. Elle's did.

Her hair was in a neat, upswept style that allowed her lovely facial features to take center stage, and made her neck look even more swanlike. He liked her neck and couldn't wait to caress it with his lips, while breathing in the warm, sweet, feminine scent of her.

He held up another cup of coffee in a takeout container. "I hope you like cream and sugar."

"I do. Thank you," she said, stepping forward and taking the coffee. She sat on the opposite end of the sofa. "Anything interesting in the paper?" she asked.

"No, the world is still in chaos and that doesn't seem to be changing anytime soon," he said with a smile. He looked her in the eyes. "How are you feeling this morning? You look lovely, but that's just the physical you. How is the emotional you?"

"Both sides of me are doing well, thanks, and you? How did you sleep?"

He gave her an enigmatic smile. "I slept like a baby."

Elle took that as a compliment, since she had sung

him a lullaby last night. She was grateful that he reminded her of that pleasant interlude, rather than her singing's-better-than-sex misstep.

She sipped her coffee as Dominic folded the paper and placed it on the coffee table. "What are your plans today?"

Elle shrugged. "I really don't have any plans. I was going to make a few phone calls and then maybe tour the city some more. There are still so many things I haven't seen yet."

"What were you going to do for lunch? Surely you'll be ravenous after all that sightseeing."

"Find a café somewhere."

"No, you're coming home with me," he said, giving her that unnerving intense look, as if he was undressing her with his eyes.

Elle looked at him questioningly and Dominic laughed a bit. "Not *my* house, my parents'. I always have lunch with them on Sunday when I'm in town. My sisters will be there, too."

Elle panicked. He wanted her to meet his whole family in one fell swoop? Couldn't he allow her to meet them one at a time instead of en masse? "I don't want to impose," she began timidly.

"You're going to meet them eventually," Dominic told her, as if it were a done deal. "My mother doesn't get to socialize with many Americans. She would love to meet you. She was born in Louisiana but she spent a lot of time in Harlem while she was with the Met."

"Oh, yeah, she was with the Metropolitan Opera when she met your father," Elle said, feeling a bit more at ease about meeting Natalie Corelli and the rest of his family.

"It was a whirlwind romance," Dominic told her. He sipped his coffee. "But I'll let her tell you about it." He reached inside his coat pocket and retrieved his cell phone. "I'm going to phone and tell her you'll be coming with me."

Elle didn't see how she could protest. She told herself that this man was offering her the chance of a lifetime, the opportunity to appear on a world stage. It would seem ungrateful to refuse to take a meal with his family. Plus, it would give her the opportunity to see how a Milano family spends a Sunday afternoon.

Dominic paused with his finger above the keys on the cell phone. "I'm dialing now," he warned her.

"Okay, I'd be delighted," Elle said, smiling.

Dominic's smile made her warm inside.

He dialed. After someone answered on the other end he spoke in rapid Italian.

Although she felt a little like an eavesdropper, Elle couldn't help hearing his side of the conversation. He laughed heartily before he hung up.

He looked at her, his eyes still dancing with laughter. "She said Gianni has already told her about you and she can't wait to meet you."

"Who's Gianni?" Elle asked, confused.

"When I got the call from the police last night I was having dinner with my cousin, Gianni. During dinner I told him about your audition."

Elle was peering into his eyes. She sensed he wasn't telling her everything. Then it occurred to her that if he was with Gianni when the police had called, then he'd probably mentioned why he had to rush off to the police station.

"Oh, my God," she said, flushing with embarrassment. "Did you tell him I'd been arrested?"

"Yes, but…"

"No buts, Signor Corelli, you either told him or you didn't."

"Yes," Dominic said regretfully, but his smile never wavered.

Elle was miffed. Was her embarrassment a source of entertainment for him? She got up and began pacing the room. "I haven't even met your mother yet and she knows I was arrested!"

"Okay, yes, Gianni told her I went to the police station because you had been arrested for hitting a policeman. That's all. Once we tell them the whole story none of this is going to matter. The cop was in the wrong, not you."

"I know that!" Elle cried. "And it's still embarrassing. I'm not going."

Dominic laughed. "All right, I can see I'm going to have to tell you the entire conversation I had with Momma. Then you'll see you have no reason to feel embarrassed." Tired of looking up at her, he got to his feet and continued. "I told her I was bringing you to lunch and she said, 'Wonderful, I can't wait to meet her. What's this I hear about her being arrested for slugging a cop? I'm sure there's a reasonable explanation. Whatever it is, it pales in comparison to what Gianni told me. He said you hired her on the spot after hearing her audition. I've never known you to do something that impulsive. Who *are* you, and where is my normally sane son?' That's when I started laughing and told her I was still sane. I would have been insane *not* to hire you."

Elle smiled because she had heard that part of the conversation. His mother sounded like a perfectly reasonable woman. Maybe she had nothing to worry about.

Dominic took a deep breath. "Now, is there any reason for you to be embarrassed?" His eyes implored her to understand.

Elle took a deep breath and sighed with the exhalation. "I guess not."

"Good," said Dominic. He turned around and picked up his coffee. "I'm going now. I'll come back for you at around eleven-thirty. You should change into something less dressy. Lunch is always a casual affair. Jeans are fine."

He was about to kiss her cheek when he seemed to think better of it and turned away.

Elle was disappointed. She could almost taste that phantom kiss.

"Tease!" she said under her breath as she watched the door close behind him.

Outside in the corridor, Dominic was still smiling. He didn't know what it was about Elle Jones that made him want to be near her as much as possible. Hadn't he just vowed, last night, to try not to be alone with her anymore, since she'd put a crack in his resolve to remain aloof where love was concerned? And then only a few minutes later he had found himself asking her to sit in on the auditions next week for male lead in the opera. To top it off, he'd just invited her to lunch at his parents' villa.

If this was a competition between him and Elle the score would be Elle Jones, two, and Dominic Corelli, zip! He had to admit, though, even if she was beating him badly, he was having the most fun he'd had in a long time with a woman outside of the bedroom.

His phone rang as he took the elevator to the lobby. He eyed the name on the screen with a bit of regret. It was Angelica. She was known to phone him on Sundays to see if he wanted to come over to her place after lunch at his parents'. She knew of that long-standing appointment, since they had been seeing one another for three years now. Dominic never took women home with him. He didn't want them to think they meant more to him than someone simply to have fun with. Nor did he want his parents to get the wrong idea. Especially his mother, who had been dropping hints lately that it was time he found someone special and started having grandchildren for his father and her. They weren't getting any younger, she complained, and wanted to have the energy to spoil the bambinos.

He answered. "Angelica, ciao, *come stai?*"

"You mean *where* am I?" said Angelica, her voice dripping with desire. "I'm soaking in the tub, alone. You want to come over later and dirty me up again?"

Dominic had been working so hard lately he hadn't accepted one of Angelica's Sunday invitations in over two months. He didn't flatter himself that she went without company when he declined. Angelica's little black book was probably thicker than his.

He had no desire to drop Elle off at her hotel later on and rush over to Angelica's apartment, though, so he gently declined yet again.

"I'm sorry, I have to work."

"Too bad," she purred. "I'm feeling a little Dominic-deprived. But I won't whine."

That's what was good about Angelica. She knew the

score. She played by the rules and when the game plan changed, she rolled with the flow. He loved women like her.

"Perhaps next time," he said. "Enjoy your bath."

"I always do," said Angelica and hung up.

Dominic put his phone away. He realized that if Elle Jones hadn't come into his life, he would have accepted Angelica's invitation.

He panicked. Having no desire to be with another woman was one of the first signs that you were getting too emotionally entangled, wasn't it? He needed to be more on guard. That one had snuck up on him.

I am not going to fall for Elle Jones, he thought emphatically.

"Benvenuto!" cried Carlo Corelli as he grasped Elle by the hand and pulled her inside the villa's foyer. Elle couldn't help smiling. Carlo's dark eyes were alight with laughter and he looked like an older, slightly shorter Dominic. He had the same color of eyes, the same Roman nose and square chin. The only difference was that Carlo's skin was the color of toasted almonds and Dominic's was closer to mahogany.

"Thank you. It's wonderful to meet you, Mr. Corelli," Elle said, smiling warmly.

Carlo offered her his arm, which she took, and he led her farther into the house, all the while looking into her eyes as though she were the most amazingly lovely creature ever to grace the planet. Now Elle knew where Dominic got that unsettling stare of his. Coming from Carlo Corelli, though, it wasn't nearly as uncomfortable.

Dominic closed the door and followed them inside.

"Hello, Dad. Your son is also here to visit," he said in Italian.

Carlo looked dismissively over his shoulder at his son. "I see you all the time," he answered in English for Elle's benefit. "But seldom is our home blessed with the presence of a goddess such as this."

Elle laughed. "I'm beginning to think you're laying it on a bit thick."

Carlo chuckled. "And she's modest, too." He looked at his son. "Why haven't you brought her for a visit sooner?"

"Didn't Momma tell you whom I was bringing to lunch today?" Dominic asked, suspicious. It appeared his dad thought he was dating Elle.

"After she said you were bringing someone to lunch, I quit listening," his father admitted. He smiled at Elle. "He never brings anyone to lunch, so this is a day to be celebrated."

Elle, grinning, looked back at Dominic. "Are you going to tell him, or should I?"

"You do the honors," said Dominic.

But Elle got distracted by the grand house. They were walking down a wide hallway on the way to the kitchen. Elle admired the marble floors, the colorful paintings on the walls and the family antiques that were everywhere.

"This is a beautiful house!" Elle said, looking up at Carlo.

Carlo smiled his thanks. "It's nice in the summer, because all the marble and the thick walls keep us insulated and cool, but it's a freezer in winter."

"I wouldn't mind freezing here," said Elle.

Dominic looked on wonderingly. She had his father wrapped around her finger.

"Who's freezing?" asked a feminine voice as they turned the corner and entered the kitchen. The room was spacious, warm and inviting. Elle loved it on sight. The double ovens and Sub-Zero restaurant-size refrigerator were stainless steel. The color of the granite countertops was deep red and the floor was a sandstone tile. A large country table stood in the center of the room, already set for eight with white linen napkins, white ceramic plates, silver flatware and crystal goblets. Fresh roses in various shades were set at strategic places around the room.

Elle, looking up at the woman who had spoken, suddenly was speechless. She had met some of the most talented singers working today, but she had never met anyone who was a legend in her own time. Natalie Davis-Corelli's performances were held up as perfect examples of what mezzo-sopranos should aspire to. Elle had never seen Natalie in a live performance, but she had studied her taped performances as if they were holy scripture for striving opera singers.

Carlo stepped aside as the two women moved toward each other, neither of them speaking, but guided as if by a mutual understanding that the things they had in common automatically made them fast friends.

Natalie hugged her and held her at arm's length to get a good look at her. "I must say, my son certainly wasn't exaggerating. You're adorable."

Elle blushed and tried to ignore the compliment. "Signora Corelli, I've seen every taped performance you've ever done. And I have all your CDs. I'm thrilled to meet you."

Natalie laughed. "Oh, God, a fan. I haven't seen one of these up close in ages."

Carlo laughed, too. "You teach at La Scala's performing arts school. You see fans every day, *cara mia*."

"Yes, but none from my old stomping grounds." She led Elle over to the table, where she gestured to a chair. "Sit down. Tell me all about yourself." Elle sat and Natalie sat down across from her.

Elle thought Natalie Corelli had certainly retained her youthful appearance well. Her dark brown skin was smooth and barely creased at laugh lines and eye crinkles. She wore her hair, black with silver shot through it, in dreadlocks. Her tall body was in shape and she wore a pair of fashionably cut jeans that Elle and her friends would have loved to be able to wear so comfortably. The purple cotton tunic she wore was the perfect color for her rich brown skin. She was barefooted, and her toenails were painted red. She was a woman totally at ease and yet she was extremely sharp and well put-together, just like her husband and son.

Elle supposed when a family had been in the clothing manufacturing business for years it was natural for them to develop a keen sense of style.

While Natalie and Elle sat at the table, Dominic was checking out the pots on the stove. "What are we having, Papa? I'm starved."

Carlo did the bulk of the cooking in their household. Natalie referred to herself as his sous-chef, his assistant. He had all the family's Italian recipes in his head. Natalie sometimes got homesick for her own mother's recipes and would cook soul food on occasion.

"Seafood stew," said Carlo. "I found some wonderful

shrimp and scallops at the market, and clams from Scandinavia."

Dominic lifted the lid on the big stew pot and breathed in the mouthwatering aroma of seafood in tomato sauce and savory spices. "What?" he said to his father. "No crusty bread?"

"You know I always make bread," said Carlo.

At the table, Elle was telling Natalie about being in the chorus at the Met. Natalie shook her head sympathetically. "I know," she said. "It's hard to get out of the chorus. No matter how good you are there is this old-school rule of having to pay your dues. But if you're smart, you get out of it by hook or by crook! No one wants to stay in the chorus unless they simply lack ambition. Good for you, coming to Milan and auditioning for Dominic. That shows initiative and an adventurous spirit. Believe me, you need both to survive in opera."

Elle was so glad to hear her idol say that. In New York, she had been beginning to think that she would never get out of the chorus. In fact she'd been getting desperate. "I was grateful to be working, but no one wants to stay in the chorus forever! I would go on auditions for lead roles and never be chosen. I was beginning to doubt my abilities."

Natalie nodded sympathetically. "Being artists we are sometimes emotionally fragile, especially after so many rejections. But you must never lose faith in your abilities, my dear. When that happens, your performances start to suffer. After all, we sing how we feel. We convey those emotions in our singing."

Elle was hanging on her every word. It was so good to talk with someone who understood her world. She glanced over at Dominic, who was sticking a piece of bread into the stew. He ate it with relish and gave his father a thumbs-up.

Carlo laughed. "It's official, then. The stew is ready."

Natalie followed Elle's line of sight and saw the way she was looking at her son. Natalie smiled. She liked Elle. But, then, she had figured she would from the moment Gianni had told her that Elle had struck a police officer. The girl was undoubtedly defending herself. Natalie admired women who weren't afraid to stand up for themselves.

"They always argue over how the food should be cooked," she said of Dominic and Carlo. "Carlo taught all of the kids how to cook. However, Dominic was the only one who showed any real interest. I think the girls thought it was expected of them, as girls, to know how to cook, so naturally they rejected the notion." She smiled. "How about you—do you cook?"

"I learned from my grandmother. She started me out peeling potatoes when I was three and, by the time I left home for college, I pretty much knew my way around a kitchen," Elle said with nostalgia. She missed her grandmother.

"Excellent," said Natalie. "One day you and I ought to whip up a soul-food feast for everyone." Without allowing time for Elle to respond to that suggestion, Natalie continued, "What about your family? Is your grandmother still around to see her granddaughter debut at La Scala?"

"No, we lost her around the time I entered Juilliard. Two years later my grandfather passed away. The only immediate family member I have left is my mom."

"No father?"

"I never knew my father," Elle told her, looking her in the eyes. They would find out sooner or later. "My mother got pregnant with me when she was a senior in high school. The boy, a football star, didn't support her and even denied having done the deed."

Natalie gave a sad sigh. "What a shame. But your mother had the support of her parents."

"Oh, yes, even though they weren't pleased about it. My granddaddy was a minister," Elle said, laughing. "My mom, Isobel, said he almost had a heart attack when she told him. But then he sat her down and had a long talk with her and, by the end of it, she was crying and he was crying. He told her that it wasn't up to him to forgive her—it was up to her to forgive herself and get on with her life without the support of the boy who'd gotten her in that fix. She had to be strong for herself and the baby. She was. With my grandparents' support, she went to college and got a degree in accounting and today she does really well for herself."

"She never married?"

"No, she has trouble trusting men," Elle revealed plainly.

"Who wouldn't, after what she's been through?" said Natalie.

Suddenly, a shrill scream split the calm of the house. "Dominic's car is here! Where is that too-busy-to-come-see-his-sister brother of mine?"

"That would be Ana," Natalie explained to Elle. "She's our youngest and if she's here that means her sister, Sophia, and cousin Gianni and his wife, Francesca, can't be far behind. Sometimes I think they travel in packs."

Elle looked up. A tall, slender and lovely young woman with long, straight black hair entered the kitchen, followed by yet another beauty, shorter and more full-figured, who wore her long, natural black hair in braids. Behind her was a good-looking Italian man around Dominic's age, bearing a toddler in his arms and holding hands with another Italian beauty whose hair fell in dark, lustrous waves with golden highlights.

Elle was in the midst of the Corellis.

Chapter 6

Everyone was talking at once. Elle, the only one who wasn't a Corelli, felt like the odd person out. She tried to follow conversations that switched back and forth between English and Italian. Although the family's interaction appeared chaotic, there were a lot of hugs and kisses and it was heartwarming to watch. An only child, Elle had sometimes felt as if she was missing something by not having a sibling or two.

After a few minutes, Dominic pulled Elle to his side and loudly said, "If everybody would be quiet for a moment, I'd like to introduce you to my new leading lady."

"What!" his sister Sophia cried. Her head whipped around so fast that the ends of her braids struck her in the face.

Suddenly everyone's attention was riveted on Dominic and Elle. Then, his sisters pressed forward.

"This is a surprise," Ana said, eyeing Elle speculatively from head to toe.

"It's more like a miracle," Sophia disagreed as she stepped in front of her younger sister to get in Elle's face. "She's too young for you, Dominic. What is she, eighteen?"

Elle laughed. "You have the wrong idea. I'm not…"

"She's American," Ana said excitedly. She glared at her brother. "Why have you kept her a secret?"

Dominic's parents and Gianni and Francesca looked on with amusement. They were all aware that Elle was not Dominic's girlfriend, but the new leading lady in his opera. It was gratifying to watch his sisters lay into him for keeping her a secret. As for Elle, she was too riveted by the drama unfolding before her to interrupt.

Poor Dominic. Even though he was much bigger than his sisters, could barely hold his own when they got upset with him. Ana was pointing an accusing finger at him and Sophia was giving him the evil eye.

Dominic threw his hands up in surrender. "Elle was trying to tell you that she's my leading lady in the new opera, not my lady!"

"You're lying," Sophia said, tossing her braids across her shoulder with a flick of a hand. "Look at her. She's just your type."

Elle was enjoying this. She had never thought she would see Dominic Corelli sweat. He was so take-charge, so confident, it appeared that nothing could get to him. But here he was taking a tongue-lashing from his younger sisters. That must mean one thing: he truly loved and respected them. She liked him even more.

"He's telling the truth," she said, finally coming to his rescue.

"Prove it," Sophia challenged Elle.

"Look," Dominic said, "you're just going to have to take my word for it. I didn't bring Elle here to sing for her supper."

"That would be lunch," Elle joked.

Everyone laughed.

"I was speaking figuratively," Dominic countered with a smile in her direction.

"Lunch, supper—whichever. I'm hungry, so I'm going to sing," Elle said. Then she stepped back from Dominic and his nutty sisters and began singing "Ave Maria." It was Sunday, after all.

"Oh, my God!" Ana and Sophia exclaimed in unison after hearing the initial notes. They stared at Elle as if they couldn't believe that sound was coming out of her body.

Elle sang the song, not in its traditional style, but with a gospel flavor. It was the way she had sung it in her grandfather's church.

Natalie had tears in her eyes. Dominic stood smiling at Elle. His heart was beating wildly in his chest. He had never been more attracted to her than he was at this moment. She was so generous to humor his sisters in this way. He felt another crack forming in his armor.

When Elle finished, both Ana and Sophia hugged her in turn.

"Girl, you can blow!" Ana said, smiling admiringly.

"I'm sorry I was so mean to you," Sophia said in earnest. She glared at Dominic. "It's just that this confirmed bachelor brother of ours doesn't ever seem to want to settle down, and when we saw you with him we got our hopes up. Forgive us?"

"It was just a misunderstanding," Elle graciously said.

Natalie stepped forward and hugged Elle. "That was so moving," she whispered. "You've got a God-given gift. Never take it for granted."

"Bellissima!" Carlo said, kissing her on both cheeks. "The song was lovely, too."

Everyone laughed again, after which they sat down to lunch.

Elle sat between Dominic and Sophia during the meal. Sophia, who worked with her father in their garment-manufacturing business, told her it wasn't at all glamorous work.

"But I enjoy watching a garment go from an idea to a ready-to-wear item of clothing. Sometimes I can spot our clothes on the street, and those are the times I feel very proud of our contribution."

"What sort of clothing do you specialize in?" Elle asked. She knew very little about the fashion industry. She only knew what she liked to put on her body. Her friend Belana, on the other hand, was a fashion maven.

"High-end women's clothing," Sophia said, "from top to bottom." She smiled. "That's Papa's way of saying we make it all—hats, lingerie, casual, everyday clothing and the dressier fashions for formal occasions like weddings and the opera."

"Where can I buy them?"

"Oh, darling, we ship to stores all over the world," said Sophia. She lowered her voice. "But you don't have to buy them. Come to my office one day and I'll show you around and you can pick out some samples."

"Samples?" Elle asked in her ignorance.

"Pieces of clothing that we used as samples for the buyers, and we simply donate them to charity or allow the employees to take them home," explained Sophia. "They're perfectly good clothing. Brand-new and they're this season's line, so you can make out like a bandit."

"Oh, girl, you're better than a bargain basement at Saks," Elle said.

Sophia laughed. "I know!"

Feeling a bit left out, Dominic said to his sister, "Will you stop monopolizing Elle? I'd like to get a word in every now and then, too."

Sophia smiled knowingly. It wasn't for her to say, but Dominic seemed to want more from Elle than just conversation. She hoped her hardheaded brother would realize it before too long, and especially before he tried to pull that I'm-married-to-my-work thing on Elle. She liked Elle and thought she deserved more than that.

Somewhere along the way her brother had started believing his mantra about not falling in love in order to preserve his precious work. He wasn't fooling anyone but himself.

"You and Elle are going to be working together, so you'll have plenty of time to chat," Sophia said to her irritated brother. "I was just about to ask her if she's seeing anyone."

She turned to Elle with raised brows.

Elle was reluctant to mention her last boyfriend, Tony, because their breakup had been so humiliating. He was also a member of the chorus at the Met. She'd caught him coming out of a closet with a soprano backstage after a performance. She'd confronted them then and there and was told they had been planning to tell her at the end of the season that they were in love. He'd said he didn't want to hurt her, but he couldn't deny his feelings for the other woman any longer. Elle had been mortified when, by the end of their shouting match, half the chorus was standing backstage observing it all. He and the soprano were still members of the chorus.

Elle sighed now. At least this was some consolation: she wouldn't have to ever see Tony and his soprano again.

"No, I'm not seeing anyone," Elle replied, and left it at that.

"That's great," Sophia said, squeezing Elle's arm affectionately. "We'll exchange numbers and stay in touch, and one weekend we can go clubbing together. My boyfriend, Matteo, has some very nice friends who would no doubt love to meet you."

Dominic bit his tongue. If he said that Elle would be much too busy rehearsing to go clubbing with Sophia, his sister would jump on it with both feet, demanding to know why he thought he was the arbiter of what Elle did in her spare time. Oh, no, he didn't want to get into that.

He was pleasantly surprised when Elle said, "Oh, I can't promise anything, Sophia. I'm sure your brother is going to try to work me to death once rehearsals start. I may not see the light of day for some time."

Sophia smiled. "I understand. He can be a brute to work for. We'll exchange numbers, anyway. You can call me and complain about him."

Elle laughed. "That's a deal."

Dominic grunted irritably and ate a spoonful of strawberry gelato. "Women!"

Elle and Sophia laughed.

Later, they retired to the back patio. The men kicked a soccer ball around on the lawn, more than anything else as an amusement for little Gianni, who ran circles around them, whooping it up.

Elle, Natalie, Sophia, Ana and Francesca sat on lounge chairs watching the men and sipping lemonade.

"He's having a ball," Elle said of little Gianni, whose giggles were music to her ears. She loved children and wanted several eventually. She had been lonely as an only child and didn't wish the same fate on her children.

"He loves roughhousing," said Francesca. She had dusky brown skin, clear brown eyes and golden streaks in her abundant wavy brown hair. She patted her belly. "I hope this one is a girl. I don't know if I'll survive two daredevil boys."

"Congratulations!" cried Elle.

By the reaction of the other women it was obvious they were already aware of Francesca's condition.

Francesca beamed her pleasure. "Thank you. We're very happy about it." She looked at her husband and son playing on the grass. Now little Gianni had big Gianni down on his hands and knees and was riding him like a horse. She laughed. Gianni would be worn out by the time they went home this afternoon. When they put little Gianni down for his nap, big Gianni wouldn't have the energy for their special afternoon activity. She laughed with the other women. She had been looking forward to it.

"Gianni's thirty-four now," she said to Elle. "He thought we should go ahead and have another child while he still has the energy to raise one. And I agreed."

"Well, at least your mother and father will have two grandchildren," Natalie said. "I can't get my children to give us even one."

"You're not old enough to be a grandmother," Ana said, smiling at her mother.

"Flattery won't get you anywhere," Natalie returned.

"I'll give you a grandchild, Momma," said Sophia. "Just as soon as I convince Matteo to give up the notion that just because I make more money than he does, it doesn't mean he won't be the man of the house when we get married."

"Italian men," Francesca groused.

"I'm not holding my breath," Natalie said to Sophia.

"Well, you won't get any grandchildren from Dominic anytime soon," Sophia told her. "He's still convinced that if he falls in love and gets married, his muse will stop inspiring him. Mozart was married and had six kids."

"Beethoven never married," Ana pointed out.

"Both girls had music lessons when they were young," Natalie explained to Elle.

"Beethoven never married because he was gay," Sophia said, sounding very sure of herself.

"What makes you think that?" Ana cried. Next to her brother, Beethoven was her favorite composer and she prided herself on knowing everything about him.

Sophia turned to her sister and began ticking off

points on her fingers. "He never was even linked with a woman. His own friends didn't know of any affairs. All men had affairs back then."

"They still have them, my sister," put in Francesca.

Undeterred, Sophia continued. "When he died his friends found letters in his house addressed to somebody he called Immortal Beloved. Now, nobody mentioned the sex of this Immortal Beloved person. It was probably a count or some other royal whose identity needed protecting. But I'm not going to argue the point. Our brother's thinking is off. That's all I'm saying. Igor Stravinsky, said to be the greatest composer who ever lived, was married more than once. And he composed music well into his seventies. He died at eighty-seven. It could be said that being happily married helped his career. Dominic is full of it."

Elle simply sat and listened. This was better than any soap opera on TV. So, Dominic Corelli believed that falling in love and getting married would negatively affect his work. That was good to know. She didn't know what she would do with the knowledge, but it was good to know.

"What about you, Elle?" Ana asked. "Are you one of those career-and-nothing-else types?"

"No," Elle replied. "I believe you can have a personal life and a professional life."

"I do, too," said Ana. "I just haven't met the right man."

"Neither have I," Elle said wistfully.

The men, all breathing hard as if they had played in a real soccer match, invaded the patio and flopped down on chairs. Sophia got up and poured lemonade into glasses for them and handed them around. "So, the Spartans return from the field of battle," she joked.

"The Spartans were Greek," Dominic reminded her.

"Actually, the Spartans started out as the slaves of the Greeks and fought for and won their freedom from the wimpy Greeks. I think they were Italian with some African thrown in for good measure," Sophia contradicted. "After all, Africa is only a stone's throw from Italy."

"Good theory," said Dominic. "Too bad it's wrong. Sparta was a city-state in ancient Greece. It says so in the history books. And I suggest you return that Gerard Butler movie, *300,* to the video store. You've seen it quite enough. It's rotting your brain."

"Honey, it's never enough," laughed Sophia. "Sometimes that movie's better than a date on Saturday night."

Elle laughed. Sophia was something else!

On the drive back to her hotel, Dominic kept stealing glances at a silent Elle. She looked pensive, as if something were weighing heavily on her mind.

"My family really liked you," he finally said.

She turned to smile at him. "I liked them, too," she said.

"Good, because I'm sure Sophia is going to make good on her threat of taking you clubbing to meet men. She loves to dance."

"How about you? Do you dance?"

Dominic was experiencing the effect again of being turned on by the sound of her voice. In the confines of the car her voice was so intimate that he felt as if it were caressing his skin. As if she were gently blowing on his naked body.

"All Italian men love to dance—it's in our blood. You know, the Latin lover," he joked.

Dominic wasn't the only one whose senses were assaulted by thoughts of luxurious sensual pleasure. Elle imagined being in his arms on the dance floor, their bodies entwined. In her imagination his hand was at the base of her spine, the feel of it sending sparks of intense pleasure along every pulse point of her body.

Her nipples hardened as her imagination ripened and he pulled her close and kissed her deeply while molding her body to his.

"Elle?"

Caught daydreaming, she sighed softly and regarded him with innocent eyes. "Yes?"

"Care to share what you were just thinking?" The mischievous glint in his eyes told her he could guess what kind of thoughts had been going through her feverish mind.

"No, I don't," she said. "Care to share what you *think* I was thinking of?"

"No, not really."

"I didn't think so," she said with a smile, and looked away. She pretended to admire the passing countryside. The Corellis' villa was a few miles outside the city limits. Their route followed several winding roads that required a driver's strict attention.

Elle was glad of it because that meant Dominic had to concentrate on his driving and wouldn't be trying to engage her in continuous conversation.

She was thinking of what Sophia had said about her brother. Was that really how Dominic felt about love and marriage? Not that Elle thought she stood a chance with him.

But up until today she had been able to dream that maybe, one day, he would begin to see her as something other than a good singer.

She was so attracted to him. No, *attraction* wasn't a strong enough word. She had been attracted to Tony. What she felt for Dominic Corelli bordered on the addictive. His presence had a pull on her body, and her mind. She literally ached to be touched by him. Was it because he was so overwhelmingly masculine and just plain *hot?* Or was it because she respected his genius? Genius could be very sexy. Intelligence in a man had always been enticing to her.

She closed her eyes. Why did she always want what she couldn't have? Was that some kind of trick the gods pulled on humans just for their entertainment? She was in Italy, an ancient country where the gods had once been worshipped. Did they still linger here as spirits, causing mischief, making a mere mortal fall for someone who was incapable of returning that love?

Admiring his profile, she gave a barely perceptible sigh, filled with longing.

Stop it, she firmly told herself. *I've got the job. Be remarkable at it. Bring the house down every night. Make each show a wonderful experience for the audience. Hopefully I'll have a long run. Then I can go back to New York triumphant. But don't start dreaming that I'm going back home with Dominic Corelli on my arm. That dream's too big.*

At her hotel, Dominic parked and turned off the ignition. Elle turned to him and forced a smile. Why couldn't she shake this melancholy feeling?

"Thanks. I had a good time," she said softly.

Dominic fought the urge to reach out and gently touch her face. The gesture would be inappropriate. He smiled back instead, and said, "I'm glad."

Elle moistened her lips with a flick of her tongue, and seeing that small action was almost his undoing. He wanted to taste her. He knew it would be a flavor he would never tire of, as addictive as any drug.

But he was technically her boss now. He couldn't cross the boundaries that existed between them. "Elle, I..."

"Yes?" she asked. Was her tone as hopeful as he imagined it to be? Did she hope for more between them than they already had? The expression in her beautiful eyes was expectant. Did she want him as much as he wanted her?

He leaned forward just a little. She leaned in also. Their eyes, if nothing else, were devouring each other. Never had the temptation been so great for him to simply grab a woman and kiss her. But it wouldn't stop there and he knew it. When he kissed Elle Jones, that is, *if* he ever kissed Elle Jones, their next step would be the bedroom. He knew that with every ounce of his being.

Their mouths were just inches apart now. Dominic breathed in her essence and tried to be satisfied with just that sustenance.

Elle demurely lowered her eyes. Someone had to be strong enough to stop this nonsense. The sexual tension was thick enough to be seen with the naked eye. But neither of them was free to act on it.

"I'd better go," she said quickly and just as rapidly reached for the door's handle and got out of the car, firmly shutting the door behind her. Just like that. Dominic didn't have a chance to suggest walking her to her door. When she was gone, he leaned back on the seat, his head against the headrest.

Racked with self-recrimination, he sat there a moment, wondering why circumstances had conspired to bring a woman like Elle into his life now. Most people fell in love when they were still wet behind the ears. Then, when they made fools of themselves it was understandable. He felt like a pitiful fool.

"Uno sciocco pietoso!" he said aloud.

Chapter 7

"Elle, wake up!" her mother's insistent voice called.

Elle sat bolt upright in her bed in the hotel room. It had only been a dream. She glanced at the alarm clock on the nightstand. It was 7:00 a.m. She'd set the clock for seven-thirty.

She didn't know why her dreaming brain would sometimes awaken her the way her mother used to wake her up for school. But if she had a pressing appointment that day, it sometimes happened. The dream would awaken her a few minutes before her alarm clock sounded.

"Weird," she murmured as she moved the covers aside and sat on the side of the bed.

Today was Monday and she didn't want to be late for the auditions.

Last night, Dominic had phoned to say she would

be riding with him to the theater in the morning. He hadn't asked, he'd simply stated a fact. Elle hadn't liked his making decisions for her, however small, and had told him she would get there under her own steam. She would be living in Milan for a while and needed to be able to get around the city on her own.

She didn't think he was too pleased with her declining his offer. He'd sighed and said, "Very well, if that's what you want. We'll be starting at nine."

"*A domani,* Signor Corelli," she had assured him.

"*A domani,*" he'd replied and then abruptly hung up.

Later that night, for the first few minutes after getting in bed Elle had tossed and turned, wondering if she had displeased him for no good reason. He'd called as a courtesy, after all. There was no rule stating that the director of the opera had to be available to offer his lead singer a lift to the theater.

However, after a while she decided that she had done the right thing. She didn't want to become dependent on him. And she certainly didn't want him thinking she was too naïve to look out for herself in this city of 1.4 million. This was small potatoes compared to NYC.

She showered and dressed and stopped at a café for a quick breakfast of a roll and a cup of coffee, then walked to the theater. She was glad that when she, Belana and Patrice had planned their visit to Milan they'd chosen a hotel in the middle of all of the most interesting sites. La Scala was only a few blocks from her hotel.

She was greeted by the doorman and told him she was here to see Signor Corelli. The short, stout, middle-aged gentleman smiled warmly while gesturing to the stairs. "He's in the uppermost balcony, in the first box, sitting in the dark, more than likely." He teasingly pointed to his head and twirled his finger in the universal sign that the person he was speaking of was crazy.

Elle laughed softly and said, *"Grazie."*

She found Dominic exactly where the doorman had said he would be, although the room wasn't dark. *"Buon giorno,"* she called as she entered.

Dominic was standing at the balcony, looking down onto the stage. Below, Roberto was explaining to thirty or so tenors how the day would progress. They each had four minutes to sing a song of their choosing, and there would be no piano accompaniment. Some grumbling was heard after that announcement.

Dominic turned toward Elle at that moment and didn't see how Roberto had handled the grumblers. His breath caught in his throat at the sight of her. Once again he was confronted by the fact that she was singularly more beautiful than his image of her in his head.

She was wearing an off-white pantsuit and the dark caramel shell underneath matched her pumps. Her hair was upswept in that style he liked so much, and she was carrying what looked like a backpack she might have used during her college days.

Elle saw him looking at her backpack. "Comfortable shoes and casual clothing, just in case I had overdressed." She remembered that the first time she had seen him, which was after her audition, he was wearing a suit. She thought she would dress similarly. *Smart move,* she thought, *he's dressed for success again today.*

"You look perfect," he said and meant it.

Elle smiled at him and walked farther into the room. "Thank you. You look great, too." She put her backpack on a chair and went to join him at the balcony. Peering down at the assemblage below, she observed, "They don't sound pleased."

"Roberto told them there would be no piano accompaniment today and some of them weren't happy about it," he said softly, his eyes on her instead of the tenors downstairs.

She laughed shortly. "They're bigger divas than the divas were."

Dominic smiled. He had to agree. The sopranos had been real troupers. According to Roberto they had been gracious to a fault, and Dominic remembered their reaction to Elle's performance. They had been generous and noncompetitive.

"You're right. I hope they remember to behave professionally today. *Mi scusi.*"

He dialed Roberto's number. After Roberto answered, he said, "Signorina Jones has arrived. You can begin as soon as you like."

"Okay, Dominic," Roberto said.

Dominic put his phone away and gestured to one of the red upholstered chairs. "Have a seat," he told Elle.

Elle, unaccustomed to his routine, said, "You won't be able to see the performances from way back here."

Dominic explained his method. "This way I'm not tempted to give the audience eye candy instead of a quality voice."

"I see," Elle said. She sat down.

Dominic walked over to a coffee service set on a nearby table. "Coffee?"

"Yes, thanks, cream and sugar."

"I remember," he said and began preparing two cups of coffee.

Shortly after he sat down next to her, handing her a china cup on a saucer with a tiny spoon on the side, the first tenor raised his voice in song.

Elle and Dominic sipped their coffee as they listened intently. Elle listened with her ears, but her eyes kept drifting back to the man at her side. How did he manage to look so pulled-together from head to toe and yet maintain such a masculine persona? Among her friends in the United States jokes were routinely made about any guy who paid too much attention to his appearance. If he dressed too well, had manicures and pedicures and made sure his hair was just so, he was said to be a metrosexual. Other males joked that it was only one step from being not truly male at all, but some freakish cross between a male and a female.

Dominic was very well groomed and no one could call him anything but masculine.

The first singer finished and she noticed Dominic taking notes. He turned and met her eyes. "What did you think of him?"

Elle was hesitant to say how she really felt. She didn't want to insult anyone. She didn't even know the tenor's name. Perhaps he was a national hero or something.

"He was…enjoyable," she said.

"*Uno* fiasco," Dominic stated flatly.

Elle cringed and nodded in agreement. "Yes, I'm afraid so."

Dominic laughed. "There is no one in here except the two of us. Don't hold back. Be brutally honest. I want your real opinion."

"Okay," Elle promised.

Of the next tenor's performance, she said, "I didn't *feel* anything when he sang. He has the technique down, but not the passion."

Dominic was impressed. He looked down at the two-word note he'd made on that particular singer: No passion.

Two hours later they were nearing the end of the line. Elle had not been moved by any of the singers. Dominic had found two of them adequate but had not been excited enough about either of them to get up from his seat and glance at them. He had recognized a few of the voices without having seen the singers. He had a good memory for voices and he was sure he had worked with at least three of the tenors who had auditioned that morning.

Then a voice rose up from below and blew both of them away with its passion.

They looked at each other and smiled. Neither of them spoke, though, until the singer had completed Puccini's "Nessun Dorma." Then they got up and went to see who had just performed such a wonderful rendition of the song that in recent years had been made universally loved by the great tenor Luciano Pavarotti.

Weak applause could be heard from the remaining tenors in the auditorium. Elle smiled. They weren't as generous as the sopranos had been to her. They didn't want to admit they had just heard the best audition of the morning.

The tenor standing on the stage behaved as though he were being given a standing ovation. He bowed, and then spread his arms in delight, basking in the adoration due him, even though it wasn't forthcoming from his disgruntled audience.

"Gracias," he said.

"That's Jaime Montoya," Dominic said, none too happy.

Elle beamed at him. "He's wonderful!"

The tall, classically handsome Spaniard walked off the stage. Roberto, standing down the steps waiting for him, pulled him aside and said something into his ear and he took a seat in the front row. Seeing this, Dominic wondered what Roberto was doing. He hadn't phoned him and told him to ask the tenor to stay.

"Mi scusi," he said to Elle and turned away to quickly dial Roberto's number on his cell phone.

"Sì, Dominic?"

"Why is Montoya staying?" he asked in low tones, not wanting Elle to hear.

"He's the last one to audition and he was the best," explained Roberto. "I thought you might want a word with him."

Dominic started to order Roberto to tell Jaime Montoya to be on his way. However, he realized just in time that the only reason he'd reacted the way he had toward Montoya was because of Elle's presence.

Last night she had said that she thought Montoya would make the perfect Cristiano. Today's auditions had proven her right. If she hadn't sighed and declared that Jaime Montoya was wonderful, Dominic would have phoned down and told Roberto to ask him to stay.

"Dominic, are you still there?" asked Roberto.

"Sì, sì, you did the right thing, Roberto. Bring him up after you dismiss the others."

Roberto breathed a sigh of relief. "Okay, we'll be right up."

Dominic hung up the phone and turned back to Elle, who was still standing at the balcony looking down on the stage. "Roberto's bringing him up. You get to meet your Cristiano. That is, if our terms are to his liking. Montoya is known for being...difficult."

"Because he knows he's good," Elle said. "Of course, that doesn't excuse rude behavior."

"No," agreed Dominic, "it doesn't." He hoped that Elle's presence would prevent him from being rude to the Spaniard this afternoon, because he didn't suffer fools gladly.

Five minutes later, Roberto ushered Jaime Montoya into the room. Elle stood back and allowed Dominic to shake the tenor's hand in greeting. Then Dominic gestured to her and she stepped forward, a welcoming smile on her lips.

"Jaime Montoya, this is Elle Jones. If we end up working together, she'll be your leading lady."

Jaime Montoya was five eleven and fit. His skin was deeply tanned, and his thick, wavy black hair was combed back from his forehead. He was as handsome as any movie idol and Elle saw from the covetous gleam in his eye that he was well aware of his attractiveness to women. Full lips curled back from perfect white teeth as he assessed her. "Then sign me up, Maestro," he told Dominic.

Taking Elle's hand in his, he kissed it in the old-fashioned European way. "It's a pleasure to meet you, Ms. Jones."

"Likewise, Mr. Montoya," Elle said pleasantly. "You're very talented."

"Thank you!" he said. *Effusive* was the only word she could think of that adequately described his grand gestures. His eyes were lit by humor. Confidence oozed from every pore. He exuded charm and style as if they were as natural to him as breathing.

Yet, she didn't find herself attracted to him. That was reserved for Dominic Corelli.

Dominic led them over to a table where three chairs were waiting for them. They all sat down and he began: "Jaime, we haven't negotiated your contract yet, but I will take your verbal agreement to be our lead tenor for now and we will proceed."

He looked back at Roberto, who quickly joined them at the table and removed two thick packets from the briefcase that he kept with him at all times. He gave one to Elle and one to Jaime Montoya.

"Just so you know," Dominic said, "there is a non-disclosure clause in your contracts. You cannot divulge the contents of those scores. Do we understand each other? The basic premise was given to the media when I announced open auditions, but nothing more. I want the audience to be surprised on opening night."

"I understand," Elle said. She was excited.

"Of course," Jaime said solemnly.

"All right," Dominic said, "first things first. Jaime, rehearsals start a week from today. Will that be a problem for you?"

"No," Jaime said, "I'm at your service."

Dominic didn't ask the question of Elle. He already knew she was on board. "Very well, then. Let me tell you a little about the story. It's set in present-day Milan. Satan is bored and he's moving among humans in the guise of a handsome young Milanese by the name of

Cristiano. One night he goes to a club and hears this young woman sing. She's an aspiring opera singer moonlighting at a blues club. In all the centuries of his existence, he has never heard a voice so lovely. He follows her home and finds out she's very poor. All the girl has are her dreams of one day becoming a famous opera singer. So because he wants her, Satan disguises himself as a music manager, Cristiano. Satan knows that if he can get her to profess her love for Cristiano then her soul is his, and if her soul becomes his he can drag her back down to hell with him and set her up as his queen. But the thing is, he falls in love with her and love is not something Satan has ever experienced. She becomes his weakness. He discloses his true identity to her and now it becomes Adama's choice. Will she continue to love him, accept his hand in marriage and spend eternity in hell? Or will she reject him and possibly face his wrath? What she doesn't know is that there is an angel watching over her, an angel who loves her. He won't allow Satan to take her to hell."

"Well, what does she decide?" Elle asked, her eyes wide with excitement.

"Read the score," Dominic said with a smile.

"It sounds very modern," said Jaime. "How many solos do I have?"

Dominic laughed. "Enough. You both are given the chance to shine." He rose and removed a business card from his inside pocket. Giving it to Jaime, he said, "Have your agent phone this number at his earliest convenience."

"No problem," Jaime said, eagerly taking the card. "My agent is standing by to hear from me."

He rose, too, and he and Dominic shook hands again. "Thank you, Maestro," he said.

"I'm looking forward to working with you, Mr. Montoya," said Dominic.

After he let go of Jaime's hand he reached for Elle's. "Ms. Jones, may I see you home?"

Observing this, Jaime's brows rose with interest. So that was how it was. The director was already playing favorites. His eyes swept over Elle once more as he backed from the room. Not that he could blame Dominic Corelli. She was ripe for the picking. A body that even Botticelli could not have dreamed up. She had a lovely face, too, and when it came to sensuality she reminded him of a young, voluptuous Sophia Loren.

"Ciao," he called from the doorway.

Dominic reluctantly drew his eyes away from Elle. "Ciao!"

Finally alone with Elle, Dominic put her arm through his and, smiling down at her, politely asked, "Would you let me buy you lunch in payment for all of your help this morning?"

Elle placed her hand on his arm. Looking deeply into his eyes, she asked, "Do you think it's wise?"

Over the course of the last two hours she had decided it was useless to keep ignoring the attraction they both felt. She wasn't a virgin. She knew when a man wanted her. She was also positive that he was aware she returned his feelings. After all, the pheromones were *kickin'*.

Dominic smiled. "Oh, are you referring to the fact that every time we get in close proximity to each other, we both wind up hot and bothered?"

"That would be it, yes," Elle said, smiling up at him.

"Do you have any suggestions for how we're going to handle this? We're going to be working together on a nearly daily basis, and you're the director and I'm the singer and never the twain shall meet." She cocked her head to the side, awaiting his answer.

Dominic loved the way she was giving him attitude. "A lot of cold showers?" he said helpfully.

"I don't think that's funny," Elle said. "I need to know your rules for this situation, Signor Corelli. You have rules for everything else. So, let me have them."

Dominic cleared his throat. "All right, I make it a rule never to get romantically involved with anyone I'm working with. In my opinion it adds an unwanted level of stress to the workplace."

He turned and bent low to whisper in her ear, "But in your case I'm willing to make an exception."

Elle went weak in the knees, not to mention her feminine center instantly started throbbing. She grew wet between her legs and a soft sigh escaped from between her slightly parted lips.

Dominic's mouth descended upon hers and she instinctively wrapped her arms around his neck and pulled him closer. Their mouths hungrily devoured each other, easing the ache that both of them had been suffering through for the past two and a half hours.

Never in his wildest dreams had Dominic thought a kiss could be this powerful. He considered himself somewhat of an expert on the subject. But of course his kisses in the past had been with women he had not deeply cared for. His goal then had been physical satisfaction alone. This kiss was on a different level.

It was so intense that, as he was kissing her, he found

that the longer their mouths were locked in the act the more he wanted. He could go on kissing her and never get enough.

Damn! Elle thought. *Why did it have to be this good? I'm doomed!*

Their bodies pressed closer still and Elle suddenly felt his erection on her thigh. This might have made her come to her senses in the past, but now it only made her wetter and moan with pleasure.

Dominic gently broke off the kiss and murmured, "*Cara mia,* I want you so much but I can't. It would be wrong."

For once in his life, Dominic Corelli was putting the brakes on seduction.

"What're you saying?" asked Elle, confused. She looked at him with eyes made drowsy by longing, her hand on his chest. Dominic removed her hand and stepped backward.

"You don't know the opera world in Milan, Elle. If anyone found out we were lovers you would be vilified in the press. Oh, they would think the man was only acting on his macho tendencies, but you would be labeled a tart, an opportunist, or much worse." He looked at her with regret. "I should have known better than to act on my feelings for you. But I've wanted you since the first time I laid eyes on you, and I've burned for you ever since. I was weak, I'm sorry."

Elle put some distance between them and turned to face him. "So, what does that mean? We will work together but avoid touching each other? We will see each other every day but be forbidden to think of how much we want each other? Is that it? I'm supposed to be strong?"

"For the time being," he said, his voice hoarse. He was not feeling very strong at the moment. Every part of him wanted Elle back in his arms.

"I don't think I can do it!" Elle burst out, frustrated.

"It's for you that I suggest this, Elle. This is your chance to be recognized as the phenomenal singer you are. We can't do anything that would get in the way of that."

Elle stared at him a moment in disbelief, then she grabbed her backpack and fled.

"Elle!" Dominic shouted in anguish. He followed. "Please don't go like this."

When she reached the stairs, Elle turned back around. Her face was tear stained, but when she looked at him it was with sober eyes. "I understand one thing, Dominic Corelli—this is simply more proof for you that love would get in the way of your work. In the future I would appreciate it if you wouldn't play with my emotions!"

Dominic wanted to tell her he was not playing with her emotions, that he really was looking out for her best interests. But this would work out well for him. If she was angry with him throughout rehearsals and the production of *Temptation,* then there would be no chance of them being caught in a compromising situation.

After the opera debuted, he would confess everything. But for now, let her be angry with him.

Looking contrite, he said, "It'll never happen again."

"Good," she told him, feeling justified in her anger. "Then we understand each other."

She turned and hurried down the stairs.

He let her go. The ache in his heart returned.

Chapter 8

It took Dominic exactly seven seconds after Elle had departed to realize what she had said: she had stated that he thought falling in love would adversely affect his work. How had she known he felt that way? He couldn't recall ever telling her that. In fact, he was positive he hadn't.

As he walked back to the balcony box to retrieve his briefcase, he racked his brain trying to come up with a reasonable explanation of how Elle had found out about that.

By the time he had grabbed his briefcase and was heading down the stairs toward the exit, he'd come up with only one answer: one of the women had told her yesterday at lunch in his parents' villa.

He reached into his inside coat pocket and got his cell phone. He took a cleansing breath before dialing his mother's number. If anyone would know, she would. She kept her eyes and ears open.

Natalie answered on the second ring. She never kept her children waiting, thinking it might be an emergency, since none of them was the type of caller who phoned simply to pass the time of day. When they called, it was for a specific reason.

"Dominic, what is it?" she asked, her tone concerned.

Dominic didn't want to go into the fact that he'd just kissed Elle and she'd blown up at him and accused him of playing with her affections. That subject was too personal to discuss with his mother. Instead he said, "Calm down, Momma. I haven't been in an accident or anything. I was just calling to ask you what you thought of my new leading lady. What are your impressions? Did she get along with you and the girls? You all looked fairly comfortable with each other."

"What's the matter?" his mother asked, instantly suspicious.

"Nothing's the matter. I just wondered what you thought of Elle."

"I'm your mother. I know when you're lying, which, by the way, you've never been very good at. Sophia takes the prize for that. She can lie to you and look you straight in the eyes without blinking. If she were ever a spy, the enemy would never get any useful information out of her. You and Ana, on the other hand, are terrible liars. I like Elle. We all do."

Now Dominic understood. "How much do you like her?" he asked. "Enough to do a little matchmaking behind my back?" That was it, he decided. His mother, his sisters and Francesca had all talked him up to Elle yesterday. Because they were women and women stuck together, they had felt obligated to warn Elle about his drawbacks and faults. Women were always trying to fix a man, make him a better person through their gentle influence. Yes, they would want Elle to know that he was convinced love would get in the way of his career. Then she would be armed with knowledge and could plan her approach with more effectiveness. Women were wonderful strategists. Generals commanding armies all over the world could use them on the front lines.

Natalie laughed softly. "Is that what you think? I stopped trying to fix you up years ago, Dominic. As for Sophia, Ana and Francesca, they have more important things to do than to try to get you to do something you have no interest in whatsoever! Like I said, we like Elle. We wouldn't want her to get involved with a man who won't return her affection. That means you, my darling son."

That hurt a little, but it was also a relief to hear.

"In fact," his mother continued, "if I'm not mistaken, Sophia brought up your belief that work and love and family don't mix. She and Ana got into some asinine argument about composers who were married and still managed to produce beautiful music, as opposed to Beethoven, who never married."

Dominic was standing on the street in front of La Scala at that point. He looked up at the cerulean sky and wished that the ground would swallow him up. His own family had stabbed him in the back and they weren't even aware of it. Elle truly believed that she meant nothing to him and he'd only used her as a convenience. *But it isn't as if we made love,* he told himself. *It was just a kiss.* Even as he thought it, he wasn't convinced. That hadn't been just a kiss. It had been the most wonderful kiss in the world.

"Momma," he said into the phone's receiver, "I've got to go."

Natalie knew by the tightness in his voice that he was upset. "Oh, no, did we inadvertently say something we shouldn't have? I'm sorry if we did. We were just talking."

Dominic sighed tiredly. "You didn't do anything. It was Sophia. She's always sticking her nose where it doesn't belong."

"Tell me what happened. Maybe I can help," Natalie suggested worriedly.

"There's nothing you can do," Dominic told her. "I've got to talk to Sophia. Ciao."

He hung up before his mother could protest.

Raising an arm, he hailed a cab. Since Elle had said she wouldn't be riding to the theater with him that morning he had left the car at home and taken a cab here. It was sometimes hard to find a parking space in this area.

Once in the back of the cab he gave the driver the address of the Corelli industrial park. The huge business was housed in several buildings on a lot, with administrative offices, the manufacturing site and the largest structure, a warehouse for storage and shipping.

Dominic had spent his summers learning the business. But finally, when he was twenty-one, his father had accepted that his calling was music and began grooming Sophia to take over their garment enterprise when he retired.

Dominic directed the driver to the administrative offices. With a grim set to his jaw he paid the cabdriver and got out.

Sophia's office was near the front of the building. She had the door open and was sitting behind her desk, the phone to her ear, when he walked in. She smiled at him and pointed to a chair in front of her desk, inviting him to sit and wait while she finished her business call.

Dominic was too wound up to sit. He paced the room. Then he heard her say, "I love you, too!" and he knew she was not talking with a client, but Matteo.

Dominic grabbed the phone and spoke into the receiver. "Hello, Matteo, this is Dominic. She'll call you back!"

He slammed the phone down so hard he nearly broke it.

Sophia, mouth open in shock, sprang out of her chair. "What's wrong with you?"

"Nothing's wrong with me that you can't fix, obviously!" Dominic yelled, glaring at her. He had the presence of mind to close the door. His sister looked at the door then back at him as if wondering if she could make it past him to leave without him grabbing her. He figured he must look like a madman to her, but he didn't care.

She stared at him with an scornful expression on her face. "I repeat, what's wrong with you? Why're you acting like a crazy man?"

"You told Elle I wasn't interested in love, that I avoided it like the plague!"

"Well, did I lie?" Sophia defiantly asked. She sat back down and calmly put her boot-clad feet up on the desk. She was wearing a pinstripe pantsuit and white silk blouse. All that was missing from her masculine attire was a tie.

Dominic continued to pace. "This is exactly why Matteo won't marry you—you're too bossy. You think you know what's best for everybody. Surely you didn't think your talk with Elle would do anybody any good."

"Certainly not you," said Sophia, her dark eyes looking straight into his. "What happened, Dominic? Did you make love to her and realize she means more to you than you thought, and panic? You *would* panic because you don't want to face the truth—your theory of avoiding love is preposterous! Not only do you want it, you need it. Love inspires, it doesn't destroy." She took a deep breath. "And as for the reason Matteo won't marry me, it's because he's too pigheaded to realize that it doesn't matter if the woman brings in more money or the man does. It's the quality of the love in the relationship that counts. He'll get that one day and then he'll marry me. You'll see."

"You shouldn't have done it," Dominic reiterated. "Now Elle thinks I used her."

"Didn't you?" Sophia asked, relentless.

"We didn't make love," Dominic told her. "We only kissed and then I realized that I shouldn't have even done that. She's in a vulnerable position. A new singer on the cusp of stardom. The least bit of scandal could ruin her. Yes, I wanted to pursue a relationship with her but it would be bad for her right now. That's what I tried to tell her, but she had been fed your rhetoric and didn't want to listen to what I had to say."

Sophia stood up, regret evident in her expression.

"Oh, God, I'm sorry, Dominic. I truly didn't mean to cause trouble. I just saw the way she was looking at you and I knew she was heading for heartbreak. I was trying to save her the pain. Now look what I've done!"

Tears pooled in her dark eyes and Dominic looked on helplessly. He'd never been able to watch his sisters cry without offering a shoulder to cry on. His anger dissipated at the sight of her watery eyes. He pulled her into his arms.

"Come now, you're a big, tough businesswoman. Cut that out!"

Sophia laughed and pushed back to look up into his eyes. "I'm not as tough as I pretend to be." She sniffed. "So, are you falling in love with Elle?"

"Can you keep a secret?"

"Obviously not!" his sister said with a short laugh.

"Then you're just going to have to wait and see, like the rest of us." He kissed her forehead and let go of her. Turning away, he said, "I've got to go. Shall we schedule another fight for next week?"

"Same time, same place?" Sophia asked softly. She was smiling now, and wiping the tears away with a tissue from the dispenser on her desk.

"I'll be here," said Dominic.

After Dominic had gone, Sophia plopped down in her chair. Her brother was falling in love, she was sure of it! She had to tell somebody. She dialed Ana's cell phone number. At this moment her sister was en route to New York City. She had left her apartment key with Sophia and told her to give it to Elle. But before she would do that, she would go to the apartment and make sure it was clean. Ana was notoriously messy, even with maid service twice a week.

* * *

Elle was so upset after her argument with Dominic that she went straight back to her hotel suite and threw herself onto the sofa in the living room, where she alternated between crying jags and spouting angry invectives against him.

She had to talk to someone or drive herself crazy!

She dialed her mother's number. As the phone rang she wondered what time it was in New York. She thought there was either a five-hour or six-hour difference; she couldn't remember. At any rate, it would be early in the morning in Harlem, which was good because Isobel got up early for work. She was at work by eight, even though she wasn't required to be in her office until nine.

Isobel Jones answered immediately. "Elle, baby girl, how are you?"

Elle sucked in a strangled breath and immediately wished she had calmed down before phoning her mother.

"I'm fine, I'm just fine. Don't let the sound of my voice make you think otherwise," she began.

"You've been crying!" Isobel said, sounding upset by the realization.

"Yes, and I feel like a fool for letting myself get so upset. You know me. I don't usually dissolve into tears at the drop of a hat. What time is it there? I don't want you to miss the train."

"It's only seven-ten, I've got plenty of time," said her mother. "Tell me what made you cry. *Now,* Elle, and I don't want any foolishness like your trying to protect me from the truth. Spill it!"

"I kissed my boss," Elle said regretfully. "I mean,

we kissed. It's not like I threw myself at him or anything."

"You told me you were attracted to him. I looked him up on the Internet. I can see why. He's very handsome. Are you sure he's not married? I don't know much about Italian men, but Louise says that back in the day Italian men used to reserve Sunday afternoons for their mistresses. You don't want to be a mistress, baby."

Elle smiled and instantly felt better. Isobel's plain way of speaking always had a calming effect on her. Growing up, she had always called her mother by her first name because that's the way Isobel had wanted it. She felt she was too young to be called Momma and over the years Elle had begun referring to her grandmother, Ella, as Mom. It was as if her grandparents were her parents and Isobel was her older sister. With only eighteen years separating them and Isobel still trying to find her place in the world, it had seemed like a good idea to put her trust in the real grown-ups. She still called Isobel by her first name, except on occasions when she let an affectionate Ma slip out.

Their relationship was that of mother and daughter, though. Isobel had never shirked her duties as a mother, always doing homework with Elle, going to all of her school plays and recitals. She'd been there for every milestone of Elle's childhood, unlike Elle's father, whose identity she knew but whom she had never met.

"It's like this," Elle said.

She told Isobel about her visit to Dominic's parents' villa and the conversation with the women on the patio. Then she told her about the kiss and her heated argument with Dominic, not leaving anything out. Not even his love-is-bad-for-you theory.

"That's a lot of bull," Isobel said about his theory. "And I can see why you said what you did to him, baby, but let's be realistic. Even though he might have been telling everybody that for years as a way to explain why he's never been in a serious relationship, that doesn't mean he believes it. We never know what's really in a person's heart. Not even your own family knows what truly makes you tick. Am I right?"

Elle admitted that she was.

Isobel took a deep breath and continued. "That's why you shouldn't have taken what his sister told you about him as gospel. Take it from me, a lot of men hide behind that excuse. Your biological father did. He was going to be a big football star and couldn't be saddled with a wife and baby. Did he do it? Who knows and who cares? The point is he used an excuse to get out of his responsibilities. Maybe Dominic Corelli is a confirmed bachelor or maybe he isn't. That's neither here nor there. What is it you're supposed to be doing over there in Italy, baby?"

"Keeping my eyes on the prize!" Elle said with conviction.

"That's right. That kiss, like he said, could have led to your downfall. He knows the opera climate over there better than you do. What you need to concentrate on is doing a good job and avoiding him, Elle. No more kisses. If you can't resist him, don't be alone with him! How many times have I sat and listened to you complain about being in the chorus and not ever being given the chance to sing a solo in an opera? Too many

times! Well, here's your chance. You can't blow it over
a kiss. No matter how good it was. Got me?"

"I do," Elle said.

She felt a lot better after her mother's pep talk.
Everything Isobel had said made sense, especially the
advice about avoiding being alone with Dominic. It was
the only way she was going to be able to resist him, and
she knew it.

"Okay," she said to her mother, "I can avoid him. But
tell me this. How do I avoid falling in love with him
from a distance? I'll be seeing him practically every
day. I can control whether or not I'm alone in a room
with him, but I can't control how my heart feels about
him."

"Honey, I have no cure for that," Isobel said regretfully.

Elle laughed. "I didn't think so, but I thought I'd give
it a try."

They changed the subject and talked a bit about her
mother's job at a firm on Wall Street and the stockbroker
who kept asking her to dinner. When Elle asked her
why she hadn't gone out with him, her mother guffawed
and said, "I'm too old for that kind of stuff."

"You're going to be forty-four on your next birthday.
That's not old!" Elle exclaimed.

"He's thirty-five."

"So, you'll be a cougar," Elle joked. "It's all the rage
these days. Heck, Cher was ahead of the curve. She was
dating younger men twenty years ago."

She had her mother cracking up. "I'm not Cher,"
Isobel said through her laughter. "I'm just an accountant."

"A very sexy accountant," Elle said. "Go out with the man, Isobel!"

"Maybe," her mother hedged.

"Promise me before I hang up," Elle insisted. "Dinner's a big step. You can start with getting a coffee with him and go from there. Go, Isobel. You might like him."

"All right, a coffee," Isobel promised. "Maybe even a short chat at the watercooler. That won't be too intimidating."

Elle laughed until there were tears in her eyes. "Okay, that's something. I'd better let you go. Have a great day. I love you!"

"I love you, too, baby. Remember to keep your eyes on the prize."

"I will," Elle vowed.

"Okay, then, 'bye, baby," said Isobel.

"'Bye," Elle said fondly.

After they hung up, Elle got up and stretched. Her stomach growled. She hadn't had lunch yet. She grabbed her purse and headed out the door. There was a nice little restaurant nearby that she liked. She would have some lunch, come back home and begin learning the score Dominic had given her. She wished she had access to a piano so that she could play the score while she sang it.

Chapter 9

"What do you think?" Sophia asked Elle after showing her Ana's apartment. The address was only half a mile from the theater. In a pinch Elle could walk to work. And the neighborhood appeared to be peopled by young professionals with children. There was a market nearby and several restaurants, all within walking distance. Elle had thought about leasing a car, but it looked like she would be able to get by without one. If she needed to go someplace that wasn't within walking distance, she could hail a cab or take the train.

It was Wednesday afternoon, and Sophia had phoned her an hour ago. She'd told her she was coming over and to pack her things because she was moving into Ana's apartment tonight. Elle was glad to hear it. She really didn't feel like imposing upon Belana's father any longer, even though he'd told her when she'd spoken with him over the phone to stay at the hotel as long as she needed. Elle balked at running up the bill any higher, even though he was a millionaire several times over. She didn't want to be beholden to him more than she already was.

When she'd told him that, he'd laughed and said, "You're like a daughter to me. You can pay me back by bringing down the house at La Scala. I'm coming to opening night with Belana. I'm telling all my friends to come."

"Thank you! I'll try not to let you down," Elle had said with a smile.

"I know you won't. Now, I've got to run. Don't bother me with talk of a hotel bill again. 'Bye, Miss Opera Star."

"Goodbye, Mr. Whitaker."

Now she turned to smile at Sophia, who was regarding her with raised brows, awaiting her opinion of the two-bedroom apartment. "I love it!"

What was there not to love? It had beautifully polished hardwood floors and was fully furnished in shabby-chic style. Good, solid furniture was upholstered in primary colors and the carpets' shades were muted. It all went together well in a modern hodgepodge.

Plus, there was an upright piano in the back next to the balcony doors. Elle walked over to it and played a few notes.

"Dominic had that delivered," Sophia told her. "He said you played and might find it useful."

Elle's heartbeat sped up at the mention of his name. She hadn't spoken to him since the incident. She imagined he was giving her space. "That was very thoughtful of him," she said to Sophia.

Sophia walked over and opened the balcony doors. A slight breeze blew in and on it the smell of something delicious cooking. Sophia sniffed the air and said, "That smell makes me hungrier than I already am. I missed lunch today."

She turned back around and looked at Elle, who still had her hand on the piano keys but had not played any more notes. She looked sad to Sophia and she was dying to ask her why. But after her argument with Dominic she had resolved not to stick her nose in his business again. That meant not asking Elle questions about their relationship.

She looked around the apartment. She'd had a cleaning service come in and go over it with a fine-tooth comb. The air was clean and fresh and the walls, ceilings and floors were immaculate.

She and Elle had brought in Elle's belongings, which consisted of two large suitcases filled with clothes and several shopping bags filled with everything she had purchased while in Milan.

Elle was in a pensive mood. Sophia decided that maybe she should just give her the key and go, before her empathy got the best of her and she wound up asking questions.

She walked over to the foyer table where she had left her purse and got the apartment key out of it. "Here's the key, Elle. Ana has it set up so that the utilities are taken care of automatically every month. And Dominic made sure that the rent was included in your contract. So, you're set. You've got my number if you should want to talk about anything. *Do* you want to talk about anything?"

Elle smiled at her. "I'm not very good company

today, am I? I'm sorry. I guess I've got a lot on my mind."

"Like what?" Sophia prodded her.

Elle sat down on the piano bench and peered up at Sophia. "What am I getting myself into? Am I as good as your brother thinks I am? Will I succeed, or will I fail?"

Sophia walked over to a chair near where Elle was sitting. She sat down and sighed softly. "Dominic wouldn't have hired you if he didn't think you were up to the task. He's obsessed with his work, a perfectionist to the bone. When he heard you sing and then looked at you, you *were* Adama in his eyes. So quit wondering if you have the talent to do what will be asked of you. Whether you'll succeed or fail is entirely up to you. I say you'll be the biggest star to perform at La Scala since Pavarotti."

"Is that a fat joke?" Elle asked, pretending to be aghast.

"Never!" Sophia cried indignantly. "I worship his memory like every other good Italian."

"I meant myself," said Elle. She looked behind her. "I think my butt has gotten bigger since I've been in Italy."

"If it hasn't, you haven't been enjoying yourself," said Sophia, who wasn't thin herself. "No, my dear, you look great. The only skinny women we tolerate are those clothes hangers who prance up and down the runway in fashion shows."

"You're talking about your sister," Elle reminded her.

"I'm not saying anything Ana hasn't heard a million times," Sophia told her. "She's only doing it to be different, to claim her individuality. Think about it—Dominic is this musical genius. I'm a formidable businesswoman. She has to do something that she thinks defines her. She chose modeling. She's wrong, of course. What she really is, deep down, is an artist." She got up. "Follow me."

Elle followed her to one of the bedrooms. Sophia went to the closet and in it was a pile of oil paintings, all covered with thick, off-white drop cloths. She chose a large one, removed its cloth and presented the painting to Elle.

Elle took the painting and held it at arm's length in order to get a better view of it. It was a self-portrait of Ana. She marveled at the detail. The sepia-toned likeness reminded Elle of an aged photograph. There were even subtle cracks in it like the weathering a photograph gets as it ages.

"This is really good," said Elle. "It looks so much like her, but why are her eyes so sad?"

"Because that's how Ana feels about herself," Sophia said. "She's not doing what she really loves."

"She's only twenty-three," Elle said in Ana's defense. "She has time to make a few wrong turns before she comes back to this."

"That's what Momma says," Sophia told her while she bent over to remove the drop cloth from another painting. This one was of Dominic.

In it he was standing onstage at the opera, obviously receiving accolades after the final curtain. He looked so handsome in his tuxedo. He held a single rose in his hand that someone had given him.

Elle took a sharp intake of breath upon seeing the

portrait of Dominic, and Sophia didn't miss it. She smiled. "She really captured him, didn't she?"

"Yes," breathed Elle. "She did. It's like he could walk out of this painting and be here with us in this room right now."

"Spooky, isn't it?" Sophia joked.

Elle handed the painting back. Sophia was right. She felt a little spooked by how realistic the painting looked. She wondered if on some night in the future, overcome with loneliness, she might be tempted to come into this room and get this canvas of Dominic just to hold it?

She almost didn't want it in the apartment with her.

But that was too foolish to say out loud, so she smiled at Sophia and said, "Did she take lessons or is she naturally that talented?"

"No lessons," said Sophia. "Imagine how good she could be if she had lessons. But then again, some of the most successful artists were self-taught."

She put the painting away. "I'm hungry. Are you hungry? Want to go somewhere and grab a bite to eat?"

Elle did, so they went down onto the street and took a stroll in the neighborhood. When they got to a quaint family restaurant on the corner, they went in and were seated by a young man in black slacks and a long-sleeved white shirt with the cuffs turned up.

He didn't offer them menus but recited what the chef had prepared for them today.

Elle looked at Sophia across the table after he had taken their orders and left. "You're so nice to look out for me the way you're doing."

"Don't mention it, Elle. It's my pleasure," Sophia

told her, smiling. "Now that you've found someplace to live, we can concentrate on your social life."

"Oh, I don't think I'm going to have much of a social life," said Elle. "We begin work in a few days."

Sophia laughed. "Too bad. I wanted to introduce you to a friend of Matteo's. He still lives with his parents, but lots of Italian men don't leave home until they marry."

The following week, rehearsals began and Elle was swept up in the chaos that was part and parcel of staging an opera. She was introduced to the large cast and found she was familiar with some of the principal players. The chorus was mostly students from La Scala's school of the performing arts, who gained experience and volunteered for the opera to count as part of their grades.

Her understudy was a mezzo-soprano from Milan who was only a year younger than Elle.

Petite and pale with huge brown eyes and long, straight brown hair, Teresa Maldonado reminded Elle of those Renaissance masters' paintings of the Madonna she'd seen in an art gallery she, Belana and Patrice had gone to here in Milan.

Surrounded by the rest of the cast, Teresa regarded Elle shyly. "Oh, Signorina Jones, I'm honored to be chosen to learn from you. I hear wonderful things about you. Can I get you a cup of coffee or tea, or warm water and lemon for your throat?"

Elle smiled down at her. "That's very sweet of you, Teresa. But you're my understudy, not my gofer. Tell me about yourself. Where did you train?"

"Right here," said Teresa proudly. "The school has

been open since early this decade. It's fairly new, but a good school. I hear you went to Juilliard. I've always heard about it and thought it might be something like the school depicted in *Fame*. Is it?"

"If you mean, are the students as dedicated to their craft as the students in the movie, then yes. They're really serious about achieving their goals. They work very hard."

"But no dancing in the streets and bursting into song in the hallways?" Teresa asked sincerely.

"Maybe once in a while," Elle joked. She liked Teresa.

Everyone stood around chatting with one another until Dominic entered the room.

When he appeared the jovial mood among the cast members was instantly dampened. You could hear a pin drop. He didn't even have to clear his throat to get their attention. All eyes were riveted on him, including Elle's.

Today he was impeccably dressed in a navy blue designer suit. He also wore a long-sleeved white shirt with a crimson silk tie and black Italian loafers. He was clean shaven, to Elle's disappointment. She thought he looked very sexy with a day's growth of beard.

His tall, well-built body fairly pulsed with power as he paced a bit before stopping to regard them. He didn't even look at her when he began: "Welcome, everyone. You've all been chosen for a reason—I believe in your ability to translate my music into a living, breathing organism, which is what I believe an opera is."

Elle heard Teresa whisper, "I think I'm going to faint," she was so excited to be in Dominic's presence. Elle turned to look at her. She was grinning like a fool.

She didn't appear faint, so Elle returned her attention to Dominic, who was now casually sitting on the edge of a sturdy table.

"*Temptation* is part modern, part traditional. I've combined classical and hip-hop music to bring something new to the audience. I'm taking a risk but with your help I think I can pull it off." Now, he glanced in Elle's direction. "For the first two weeks, feel free to refer back to the score while we're rehearsing. However, by the third week I expect you to have learned your parts and I don't want to see any paper on the stage." He paused for a couple of minutes so that what he'd said could sink in. Then he added, "Shall we begin? Signorina Jones, you have the opening aria." He looked at the pianist, a short Italian man with a receding hairline. "Vincenzo. Music, if you please."

Elle didn't take the stage fast enough for him, so he clapped his hands with a sharp, staccato beat and cried, "Quickly, Signorina Jones!"

Elle nearly ran onto the stage. Dominic shouted, "Careful. What do you want to do, trip and break your leg? Then where would we be? The rehearsals would have to be postponed because the lead soprano would be incapacitated."

Elle didn't let him fluster her. So what if he was being an ass? She didn't care if he shouted at her all day: she was a professional. She would do her job.

Dominic cued Vincenzo to start playing. Onstage, Elle had already taken a deep breath and was ready to begin.

When the curtains rise in the first act, Elle's character, Adama, is singing in a blues club in Milan. The club is smoky. The crowd is loud and boisterous.

Adama sits on a stool onstage with only a piano player behind her to enhance her skills as a singer. The song she sings is about loneliness. She's written it herself and it's heartrending.

Elle didn't need notes. Over the past four days she had played it at least twenty times on the piano. She had saved her voice, though, until now. She felt the meaning behind the song, passionately knew how it felt to be as lonely as Adama. She looked straight into Dominic's eyes as she sang a song he had conceived on paper.

"I can't take this desolation, this black hole of misery, and I keep hoping, praying that you'll come back to me."

After she sang that last verse, Dominic had to wipe a bead of sweat from his brow and compose himself. He cleared his throat, quieting the enthusiastic applause from her fellow cast mates, and said with apparent sincerity, "Let's hope you'll do that song better on opening night, Signorina Jones." But it was a fabrication. He had loved her performance.

Elle was finally flustered. What more did he want from her? She knew the others had thought it was flawless. *I won't let him get to me!* she thought with vehemence.

Eyes narrowed, she smiled and said, "I'll work on it, Signor Corelli."

"You do that," said Dominic. Then he turned his gaze away from her and focused on Jaime Montoya. "You're next, Signor Montoya."

Jaime rolled his eyes and walked onto the stage from the wings. When he passed Elle, he whispered, "You were superb. He's a fool."

"Did you say something, Signor Montoya?" asked Dominic.

Jaime stood at center stage and bowed slightly from the waist. "Perhaps my ear for music isn't as refined as yours, Maestro. But I thought Elle's performance was perfection itself."

"I'm not concerned with your ear for music at the moment, Signor Montoya, but your voice. Let's hear Cristiano's first solo, shall we?" He smirked. "And I see you have your score with you. Good. If Signorina Jones had been able to refer back to hers maybe she would have performed better."

After Jaime's solo, Dominic said, "I was mistaken. Having your score with you made no discernible difference to your performance. Both you and Signorina Jones have a lot of work to do."

Unlike Elle, Jaime saw red. "I'll have you know, Maestro, that I'm not accustomed to being maligned by my director. I would appreciate it if you would hold a civil tongue in your head when speaking to me!" he said angrily.

"And I would appreciate it if you would start to earn the exorbitant fee we're paying you for your participation!" Dominic returned. "Civility is earned. Feel free to give as good as you get, but if you don't like the way I direct then you can always leave."

Jaime muttered an expletive in Spanish and stormed off the stage.

On the sidelines, Teresa whispered to Elle, "This is classic behavior for La Scala. We wouldn't feel at home without a bit of melodrama."

Elle smiled. Yes, she'd heard some unbelievable stories about backstage antics at La Scala. But she had hoped that things would run smoothly. It seemed that her hopes had already been dashed. As rumored, Dominic was behaving abominably when directing his operas.

Later, after Dominic had called it a day, everyone got out of there as fast as they could, except Elle, who stayed behind to have a word with him. He was packing up his briefcase, a frown creasing his brow, when she walked up to him. "Signor Corelli," she quickly said, "thank you for the piano. Sophia told me you had it sent over. Thanks also for having the cost of my rent written into the contract. That was very thoughtful. It didn't even occur to me to ask."

Dominic continued to look down and ready his briefcase for leaving. "You're welcome."

Elle stood there, looking at his bent head and wishing she were free to touch him. It hurt her that he wouldn't even look up. Were they supposed to behave as if that kiss had never happened? Couldn't they at least be courteous?

She felt tears prick the backs of her eyes, but subdued them with angry, venomous thoughts about him. Turning away, she said, *"A domani,* Signor Corelli."

"Don't be late," said Dominic in a low voice.

He looked up only after he heard the door shut behind her. Squeezing his eyes shut as though he were in pain, he threw his head back and whispered, "God, why do you make me suffer like this?"

Not that he expected an answer. He was his own worst enemy. He had been the one to kiss her, after all, thereby rendering himself defenseless against the burning memory of that kiss. Yes, it was torture of the sweetest kind.

As for his boorish behavior today, it was a necessary evil. He preferred Elle's hatred to dooming her chance at stardom before it even got off the ground.

She would forgive him later. He was counting on it. Besides, he was a firm believer in trial by fire. A lump of coal became a diamond only after years of having pressure put on it. A little pressure would be good for Elle Jones. It would either break her or make her. He believed it would make her.

As for him, a daily exercise routine of running and weight lifting wore him out sufficiently to make sleeping at night possible. He still burned for her, but he was managing. Or so he told himself.

Chapter 10

For the next eight weeks, Elle arrived at the theater on time and subjected herself to more abuse from Dominic. She had to be fair, though—he heaped abuse on everyone, not just her. The least little mistake, like forgetting a word of the lyrics, would set him off. Once one of the chorus members was off-key, and his subsequent angry tirade made the woman burst into tears and stumble from the stage, never to return.

Elle was beginning to wonder if he was insane—a genius, yes, but totally bonkers. She'd worked with directors before who were demanding, but Dominic Corelli took demanding to new heights.

Rehearsals were grueling enough without having the director behaving cruelly. First there was the music rehearsal, when the singers practiced their parts with only a piano accompaniment. Then the staging rehearsal, where the singers practiced their stage movements so that they didn't look awkward performing on a stage full of scenery. Next was the technical rehearsal, when the opera was rehearsed onstage, with the performers in costume and the sets in place. Following that was a sitting rehearsal, as the singers and orchestra performed together for the first time. Then it progressed to the orchestra staging rehearsal, where all the elements came together—the soloists and chorus members sit onstage, not in costume, while the orchestra occupies the orchestra pit. The entire opera is rehearsed from beginning to end, and the vocalists sing full out so that the director can judge how they and the orchestra sound together.

Finally, there is the dress rehearsal, the last rehearsal prior to the first performance in front of an audience.

This was the most stressful rehearsal for Elle, which was why she blew a gasket, slapped Dominic Corelli and called him the devil in front of the entire company.

When she thought about it later, it all seemed like a dream sequence to her. She and Jaime had been onstage in full costume singing their duet. Elle was melting inside the heavy brocade gown. The opera's setting went back and forth between present-day Milan and a fantasy world that Satan creates just for the two of them that looks like fifteenth-century Italy. In the duet, Elle's character, Adama, was dressed in an emerald-and-gold gown and her hair was up in an elaborate style, shot through with gold ribbons. Elle thought she looked like the Bride of Frankenstein with the wig on. She and Jaime were coming to the big ending in the duet when she tilted her head back and the wig fell off.

The players and the orchestra members alike laughed

good-naturedly as Elle bent and picked up the wig. She was putting it back on when Dominic yelled, "Okay, take it from the top. And this time, Signorina Jones, try to keep the wig on."

So she and Jaime took it from the top and the wig fell off a second time at the exact same moment.

Dominic yelled, "Must we *glue* the wig on?"

Elle glared at him. "No, but you can most certainly glue your lips shut!" she yelled back. "The wig obviously needs refitting. I suggest you give me time to go backstage and have it done. Then we can continue."

Incensed, Dominic leaped onto the stage and confronted Elle. "Are you trying to tell me how to direct this opera?"

It was the first time in weeks that Elle had been this close to him and her poor body betrayed her by reacting to his nearness. In spite of the hell he'd put her through for the past two months, she was still overwhelmingly attracted to him.

Judging from the bitter expression in his dark eyes, though, he loathed her. He was a man obsessed. No one and nothing meant anything to him except this damned opera, and she was fed up with his behavior.

"Well, are you?" Dominic yelled after she simply stood there staring at him.

Elle slapped him.

There was a collective intake of breath on the part of the shocked onlookers. "Somebody needs to!" she cried, as tears, held back for too long, spilled onto her cheeks. "You're the devil incarnate, Dominic Corelli, and I hate you!" With that, she left the stage to thunderous applause.

Dominic, laughing and holding his jaw, looked out

at the cast and orchestra members. "That, my dear colleagues, is how a diva behaves. Take five while her highness gets her wig on straight."

Later, after a successful run-through of the entire opera, Elle stayed behind to talk to Dominic.

To her amazement, he wasn't aloof or rude when she approached him as he was packing up his briefcase. He looked straight at her and smiled. "Have you come to apologize?"

Elle, who had changed into jeans, a short-sleeved purple blouse and strappy taupe sandals, said, "No. I just wanted you to know that I'm ready for tomorrow night. In the beginning I lacked confidence but, after everything that I've been through under your direction, I think I can handle anything." Her eyes flashed with anger. "I don't know whether you're a sadist, or you simply believe that being really hard on me will bring something wonderful out of me. It doesn't matter. I will *bring* it tomorrow night. You don't have to worry about me."

His smile never wavered. "I'm not worried about you," he assured her. He closed his briefcase and walked up to her. "I'm not sorry, either, Elle. It's part of my creative process and I don't feel I should have to apologize for it. Greatness is not achieved by sitting back and waiting for it. You have to struggle for it. Fight for it, and win it. You've fought for it and won it. Tomorrow night, I want you to claim it."

With that he turned and began walking toward the exit. "Get plenty of rest and remember to save your voice."

Elle watched him go. Regret weighed heavily on her heart.

Outside in the hallway, Dominic took a deep breath and leaned against the wall, then pushed away from it because he didn't want her to see him in this weakened state. He continued walking, even though all he wanted to do was go back in there and tell her he was sorry for behaving like a maniac. Explain that it was the only way he knew to ensure they would stay away from each other. She had to detest him. She had to be kept off balance. Otherwise they would have engaged in an affair that would have been detrimental to both of them. He saw the way she looked at him when she thought he wasn't watching. She still wanted him, which was good, because he most definitely still wanted her. She was constantly on his mind during waking hours and he had dreamed about her so many times he had lost count.

The excitement was palpable backstage on opening night. It was like a living, breathing entity that was bursting with energy. Elle's dressing room overflowed with flowers from well-wishers—family, friends and celebrities she'd never met, including Kanye West and Beyonce. The buzz was that both were in the audience.

Earlier that day, Elle had been swamped with phone calls and text messages from Belana, Patrice and Isobel, all of whom had a private box along with Belana's father, John Whitaker, and her brother, Erik. John had been kind enough to put up all of Elle's guests in a nearby luxury hotel. Elle hadn't spoken since last night in an attempt to preserve her voice for tonight, so she'd been using text messages to communicate. Luckily, they all understood and were going to be at the celebratory party after the show.

The wardrobe assistants had just left her dressing room and Elle was alone. She smiled at her reflection as she stood in front of the mirror. A beautiful girl who seemed to glow from the inside out smiled back at her. She felt surprisingly calm. A few butterflies, but nothing serious. She figured after laying into Dominic yesterday all negative thoughts had been banished. She *was* Adama. Elle Jones was nowhere to be seen.

"Five minutes, Elle!" yelled one of the many performing-arts-school student volunteers from outside her door.

Elle walked to the door, opened it and said in a whisper, "Thank you, I'm ready to go."

The messenger, a slender girl just out of her teens, smiled, wished Elle good luck in Italian and gave her a thumbs-up as she departed.

"Grazie," Elle said as she hurried from the dressing room and took the now-familiar route to the backstage area.

A few minutes later, the lights in the opera house lowered, the curtains opened and the orchestra began playing. She was in her element. She was where she was born to be and it showed in her performance.

After the first act, she felt she was reaching her stride. By the second, she could feel the energy of the audience in every inch of her body. This was what she liked most about live performances, the exchange of energy between the performer and the audience. She knew they were enjoying themselves, and she had never felt better in her life.

After the final act, they received a standing ovation.

There were shouts of *"Brava!," "Bellisima!"* and roses were thrown at the cast's feet. Then someone yelled from the *loggione,* the uppermost balcony for those who couldn't afford more expensive seats. The loggionisti were known for raining insults on singers they deemed unworthy. Elle remembered that they had even booed Pavarotti while he was singing *Don Carlo* in 1982. She looked up. It was Violetta, the prostitute she had met the night she'd been falsely arrested, leaning over the balcony. "You rocked the house, my sister," she yelled in Italian.

"Molte grazie," Elle shouted back, and blew her a kiss.

After the cast had been lauded by enthusiastic applause until their ears felt assaulted, Dominic walked onto the stage and the audience went crazy all over again. The cast, out of deference to him, turned and applauded him, as well.

Elle smiled. It was like Ana's painting all over again. She felt her heart swell with pride. Even if a part of her detested him, he deserved this moment. He looked handsome in his tux; breathtaking, actually. Elle sighed. Things could have been so different between them if not for his dumb theory about love.

Jaime was beside her, holding her hand. "You've got to admit," he whispered, "even though his method seems quite mad, it works. You were luminous tonight."

"So were you," Elle said sincerely.

"Thank you," Jaime answered with rare modesty. "But you don't get my meaning. You will later on, when the notices start coming out."

Elle always dreaded reviews. It seemed that the critics never understood her, or if they did they would compliment her one moment only to take it back with a dig the next. Her stomach lurched.

The curtains finally closed. They all scurried to their dressing rooms to get out of their costumes and head to the opening-night party at Hotel Principe di Savoia Milano.

In her dressing room, Elle took a quick shower and dressed in a lovely, sleeveless, pale-blue sheath that showed off her fit body and long legs. It was June and the nights got cool, so she had a wrap to put around her shoulders. She had found the dress at Corelli's warehouse when Sophia had let her loose in the sample room. On her feet were sexy sandals with three-inch heels and her purse had the same silver tones. The only jewelry she wore were silver dangle earrings in a simple but classic teardrop design.

Since this was her first starring role, Elle had no inkling of what was in store for her when she set foot outside her dressing room. The moment she opened the door, flashbulbs started going off. There were photographers waiting for her, and reporters. Behind them were a number of celebrities whom she recognized on sight. She was so dumbfounded that her first impulse was to turn and escape back into her dressing room.

But, suddenly, Dominic was by her side, pulling her close and snug next to him.

"Don't be nervous," he whispered. "You're a star now. Give them a quote or two. Smile for the cameras and then I'll get you out of here, I promise."

It was the caring tone of his voice that calmed her. It certainly was not his hands on her body.

For the next few minutes, Elle posed with Dominic for pictures. Then, because opening night at La Scala was big news in Milan, TV reporters pressed forward and began bombarding them with questions. A tall, dark, good-looking male reporter asked Dominic how Elle had happened to audition for him. "It was a miracle," he said in Italian. "She was vacationing in Italy and walked in off the street." The look he gave Elle as he pulled her closer to his side was filled with admiration. Elle glowed.

"Signorina Jones, how do you feel tonight?" asked the reporter.

"Like a fairy-tale princess whose every wish has been granted," Elle replied happily.

"Well, you certainly look like a princess," said the handsome reporter. "And you sang like an angel from heaven."

After a few more short interviews, Dominic politely let the press know that he and Elle had a prior engagement and thanked them for their generosity. Shortly afterward, Elle saw her mother and hurried into her open arms. "If only your grandparents had lived to see this," her mother breathed excitedly. "Baby, you shone like a star tonight!"

Belana and Patrice took turns hugging her and John and Erik Whitaker kissed her on the cheek. Elle couldn't help noticing that John only had eyes for her mother and wondered what, if anything, the handsome bachelor was going to do about the crush he had on her.

Then, Natalie and Carlo Corelli showed up and the kissing and hugging started all over again. Sophia was there with Matteo, whom Elle had met on several occasions in the past few weeks as she and Sophia had become good friends. Ana had flown in from NYC. Her companion was a fellow model whom she had recently begun dating.

Through all of this Dominic remained at her side, which surprised Elle but wasn't unwelcome. Soon, the party moved to a five-star *ristorante* at Hotel Principe di Savoia Milano in the city's midtown. Since the 1920s the hotel had been home away from home for the crème de la crème of society. The guests at the reception numbered in the hundreds, among them the mayor, other city officials and international VIPs, including royalty. Elle had heard that opening night at La Scala was an event, but she had never expected to shake hands with a princess or receive a kiss on the hand from the president of a country. It all felt surreal to her. If not for Dominic she didn't know how she would have handled it.

She was glad when Dominic escorted her to their private table, where her mother, his family and all their friends were already seated and getting to know each other. When she and Dominic sat down next to each other at the table they were greeted with more applause, the most gratifying of the evening since it was coming from those whom they loved.

"Enough of that," Dominic said modestly. He turned to Elle. "Unless you're not tired of it yet," he joked.

Elle laughed. "I'm with you. Let's eat, I'm starving."

"A diva never eats before a performance," Dominic reminded everyone at the table. His mother nodded with a knowing smile; she was well aware of how a diva behaved, since she was one.

Elle saw that Gianni and Francesca were at the table,

as well. She hadn't seen the couple backstage. "Hello, Gianni, Francesca, I didn't see you earlier."

"The babysitter was a little late arriving," Francesca explained.

"Also, Francesca couldn't decide what to wear," Gianni joked.

"You look beautiful," Elle said, smiling. "You both look wonderful. How is little Gianni?"

"Oh, he's well, for now," Francesca said. "Yesterday, he tried to climb the bookshelves in the library."

Gianni turned to his wife. "I told you, I thought they were secure!"

Francesca smiled at her contrite husband. Then she turned her attention to Elle. "He knocked over one bookshelf and the rest fell over in a domino effect."

"Books were everywhere," Gianni said, getting into the story since Francesca was determined to tell it.

"It scared him so badly he went and hid under the bed—he just knew he was going to be severely punished. I was laughing so hard, I couldn't summon up the energy to punish him," Francesca told Elle, laughing.

"Thank God he didn't get hurt," Elle said.

"That's what I told Gianni when I stopped laughing," Francesca said, looking accusingly at Gianni.

"The carpenter's coming on Monday, sweetheart," Gianni said in his defense. "Now, can we change the subject?" he asked, looking around the table. "I'm sure no one wants to hear about our son's misadventures."

"I don't mind," said Belana mischievously. "He sounds like my kind of kid. How old is he?"

"He's almost two," said Francesca, smiling gratefully at Belana.

"Uh-oh, the terrible twos," warned Belana. "I'm afraid you're in for more trouble."

"Send him to the army," Carlo joked. "They could use a good demolitions man."

"Yes, but he'd never make the height requirements," said Natalie. "Just let me have him for a week, Francesca. When I return him to you, he'll be so worn out he won't have the energy to get into mischief."

"Is that your sneaky way of getting free labor for your garden?" Francesca asked, grinning.

"Yes, but don't tell him that," Natalie said. "I'll convince him he's digging his way to China. Children always fall for that one."

"Just because we fell for it, doesn't mean today's kids will," Dominic said. "They're more sophisticated than we were."

"That's true," Patrice put in. "I've got a three-year-old niece who knows more about the computer than I do!"

"Honey, aren't they born computer-ready?" asked Isobel. "The way today's kids are hooked on electronics, it almost seems like they have earpieces surgically implanted. They're never without them. In fact, no one under the age of forty is ever without them. Show of hands. How many of us have an iPod or a cell phone or some other electronic device on their persons?"

Everybody raised their hands. Belana's brother, Erik, raised both his. "I've got an iPod, a BlackBerry and a digital camera on me."

"I rest my case," Isobel said. Smiling at Francesca, she said, "Your son sounds darling to me."

Elle smiled. Her mother was usually reticent about engaging in conversation with people she hardly knew.

What was happening to her? Elle had even caught her smiling sexily at John Whitaker, who had grinned widely upon seeing that smile. She'd accepted a ride on his private jet to get here. What else would she be accepting from him soon? For years she had been telling her mother that John was attracted to her. Could her mother now have decided to act on that fact?

"I'd like to know what inspired you to write *Temptation*," Patrice asked Dominic. "I've noticed that all of your operas are about the devil in one way or another. Are you obsessed with the devil?"

Dominic smiled at Elle. "According to Signorina Jones, I *am* the devil."

"He pushed me to the limit yesterday," Elle explained, "and I slapped him and told him he was the devil."

Only Isobel was aghast at this news. No one else seemed surprised by it.

"I've often thought he was Satan and I've never sung for him," Sophia teased. "He must have put you through hell."

"Oh, he did," Elle said. "He yelled and stamped his foot like an overgrown child. I suppose everyone else he works with is used to his tantrums, but I'm not. It took all my willpower not to stick a pacifier in his mouth and tell him to be quiet."

Everybody, including Isobel, laughed at this. She was relieved. It sounded like Elle and Dominic Corelli had worked out their problems. She was still worried that Elle was smitten with him, though. Also, judging from the covetous glances Dominic Corelli had been giving her daughter, he was definitely not immune to her charms.

Chapter 11

"Elle, what are you doing out here?" Dominic asked.

He startled Elle. She was standing outside on the veranda of the restaurant. After enjoying a wonderful meal she had excused herself from the table on the pretext of going to the ladies' room when, in reality, she needed some air. In spite of being surrounded by people she cared for, all of the excitement was overwhelming.

Especially after one of the hotel staff had come to their table with a fax for Dominic. It was their first review. Elle's stomach had clenched nervously as Dominic began to read:

The Devil and Miss Jones should have been the title of the latest offering from hometown boy Dominic Corelli. A delicious combination of classical music and hip-hop, *Temptation*, like anything that tempts, was impossible to resist. And at the center of this marvelous opera was the American mezzo-soprano Elle Jones, who in her La Scala debut held the stage like a seasoned singer. With her earthy, sultry voice she enticed and cast a spell upon the audience as Adama. Not since Grace Bumbry has La Scala been graced with the presence of such natural talent. Tenor Jaime Montoya gave polished, convincing performances both as Satan and as Cristiano, the devil in human guise...."

It went on and on, praising the conductor, the supporting cast and even the technical team who moved the scenery around on the stage.

Upon hearing it, the cast had celebrated by drinking champagne. Everyone had praised Elle, saying this was the beginning of a stellar career. She had felt dizzy with emotion.

Soon after that she had left the table, murmuring something about the ladies' room. But as soon as she saw the doors leading out to the veranda, she had escaped through them. Five minutes later, Dominic had found her.

The moment he stepped outside and felt the chilly night air, he removed his jacket and put it around Elle's shoulders. The garden in which they stood was lit up with golden lights strung in its trees and shrubs. The effect was very calming, almost magical.

Dominic stood behind her, not touching her except to place his jacket about her shoulders. "Is it too much?" he asked quietly.

Elle didn't turn around. She was afraid if she did, she would throw herself into his arms, seeking the comfort that he would never freely offer. "I'm sorry," she said. "It's a lot to take in. I'll be okay. I just need a few minutes alone to remind myself that I worked for this. It hasn't been given to me on a silver platter."

"That's right. You've been preparing for this all your life," Dominic told her. "Besides, we haven't gotten all the notices yet. The other critics might think you stunk up the place."

Elle laughed nervously. "One can only hope."

Dominic grasped her by the shoulders from behind. "Don't get your hopes up too high, because you were brilliant tonight, Elle. You *brought* it, as you told me you would. I've never been prouder of anyone."

He was encouraged by the fact that Elle didn't wrench free of his hold. He thought he might venture a bit further. "I had to do what I did so that you could experience this night," he said softly.

Upon hearing this, Elle turned around and peered up at him with a puzzled expression.

"I tried to tell you," he continued, "but you didn't want to hear it then. If I had pursued you before we had premiered the opera they would have said you had the lead only because you and I were lovers. No matter how fervently I denied it they would have been unconvinced. But now, Elle, if you still want me, they will say we have discovered kindred spirits in each other and that you've become my muse. It's true, Elle. No other woman has interested me in the least since I met you. I ache for you. I did then, and I still do."

Elle calmly took his jacket off and handed it to him. Thrusting it into his arms, she cried, "I can't be with a man who can turn his emotions on and off as easily as a faucet."

She turned her back on him and tried to walk away but Dominic grabbed hold of her arm. "Do you think I didn't suffer as much as you did? I had to watch you looking at me with barely hidden longing and not go to you and take you in my arms and kiss you senseless. I had to watch that pompous Spaniard flirt with you without punching him in the face. I think he got some kind of sick pleasure out of it. I was jealous every time he touched you and pretended to make love to you onstage. All of these emotions I had to stamp down because I knew that acting like a lovesick fool wouldn't do either of us any good!" he said loudly.

"Don't shout at me!" Elle shouted back at him.

"Then kiss me and shut me up!"

"Never," said Elle in a lower tone. "Shout all you want. You had your chance, Signor Corelli, and you blew it, baby. I'm not going to be another notch on your bedpost, no matter how good your kisses are."

He gave her a wicked smile. "Then you admit that was a good kiss?"

"The best I ever had. Hey, I love ice cream, too, but I know I can't have it because it'll make me fat. Same difference—I can resist you because you're bad for me."

"I beg to differ," he said confidently. "I think I would be good for you. Good for you, and good *to* you."

"You don't believe in commitment," she stammered, stating one of the reasons he would be bad for her.

"You're embarking on a new, exciting career," he countered. "What do you need with commitment? It's better if you're not tied down. With me, especially, you would have the best of both worlds—I'm in the same business, so I would understand when you had to fly to some exotic locale to sing. And, too," he said smoothly, moving closer to her ear, "I would be a lover that would satisfy all your needs, and not ask you to get up and cook me a meal afterward. As you know, I can cook for myself. No, I don't want a wife, Elle. I want an equal."

"A wife can be an equal," she suggested, holding steady.

"Come now," he gently said. "You've noticed it. The moment a man marries he becomes lax in worshipping his woman. Fewer flowers and other gifts and fewer nights on the town and, what's more, he no longer feels the need to impress her. So he leaves his clothes on the floor. He forgets to phone when he's going to be late. It's better not to marry, Elle. Let's be lovers and friends, not husband and wife."

"You're really full of it," Elle said with a short laugh. "You have examples of great marriages in your own family—your mother and father, for one. Gianni and Francesca have a hot marriage. They can't keep their hands off each other."

"And they've got one kid and another on the way as proof," said Dominic.

"What? You don't want children, either?" she asked incredulously.

"Elle," he said lazily, lowering his head to plant a kiss on the side of her neck. "All I want is you in my bed, as soon as possible."

"Oh, that's a lovely invitation," Elle said sarcastically, moving away from him. "Thank you very much, but I'm going to have to decline."

The look he gave her was one of disbelief. "You're turning me down because I don't want to get married and have children?"

"That's right," Elle told him emphatically. "I don't make love to men whose children I wouldn't want to have. Sex has consequences. My mother's experience taught me to be careful. I already know how you feel about love and family. Though, God knows, I don't know why you feel that way. Did somebody drop you on your head when you were a baby?"

Dominic laughed. "Now you've got jokes. Woman, you are truly the most impossible person I've ever had the displeasure of meeting."

"A minute ago, all you were thinking about was giving and taking pleasure," she reminded him, which irritated him further.

Dominic let out a frustrated breath. "I must have been temporarily insane."

"No, my dear Signor Corelli, you are permanently insane if you think I would touch you with a ten-foot pole, after the hell you put me through during rehearsals and your smarmy confession that love and marriage are repugnant to you!"

"So, you would never consider making love to a man who would only give you the world, not marriage and children?"

"It *is* possible to have both," she said. "And nothing you say will change my mind. I'm not settling for less than love, marriage *and* children."

"My parents and Gianni and Francesca are exceptions, Elle. The majority of marriages end in divorce. You know I'm not lying."

"No, you're not lying. You're also not showing any faith in love, either. You're a hypocrite."

"So now I'm a hypocrite, when I have truthfully stated my position for you? I didn't lie to you and say I love you and pledge faithfulness till the day I die just to get you into bed. I told you what I am willing to give in exchange for what I want from you."

"You're a hypocrite because you write such beautiful music, such wonderful stories about true love," she proclaimed. "Yet you don't believe in it."

Dominic sighed. "All right, you've given me examples of couples who are happy. For every one of those, there are single people who can't find true love. Take your mother, for example. She never married after your father let her down. My own sister, Sophia, is in love with a man who is afraid to marry her because he thinks she'll castrate him. And Ana, poor Ana, who is so beautiful men want to date her because she looks good on their arms, or to brag to their friends that they're dating a supermodel. She has yet to meet anyone who sees *her* and not her body or her beautiful face. So, I'm offering you affection. So much affection that you'll never notice that it isn't the fairy-tale love that you will spend your life looking for. Take *me,* Elle, instead of that idealized male who may never appear on your horizon. What have you got to lose? You're a young, beautiful woman who deserves to wring all the pleasure she can out of life. Take it."

That did it. *Good God, the man has a golden tongue,* Elle thought, and threw herself into his arms. He was right, so right. She wanted him now. So what if the future never brought her that epitome of male superiority that she had created in her mind?

They kissed roughly, almost painfully. The intensity of the moment dictated the violence with which they were possessed.

She hated him for making her face the truth, yet she loved him for it. She felt split in half. She was the same Elle she had been a few minutes ago, who didn't believe in settling for less than she deserved. Unfortunately, she was also the Elle who desired this man. Dominic drew her to him with his passion for life and an indefinable attraction that was so strong she couldn't resist it.

They succumbed to the tumultuous emotions they had held at bay for so long.

She felt his muscles rippling beneath his tux as her hands traveled along his back and farther down to his butt, pressing him so close to her that she felt his erection straining to be freed from his trousers.

Turning his head, he broke off the kiss and said hoarsely, "We'd better get back before we're missed. But, remember, I'm the one taking you home tonight."

"Yes," she said breathlessly. "Yes."

When Elle and Dominic returned to the reception, Jaime, who was surrounded by beautiful women at his table, called them over. His dark eyes were shining with excitement. "Look," he said, holding out another faxed sheet, which held the latest review. "The critic from *Corriere della Sera* says *Temptation* is an instant classic that will stand the test of time like Verdi's *Requiem*."

Dominic took the sheet of paper and read the review from Milan's daily paper to Elle, then he handed it back to Jaime. "It seems we are a success," he said. *Corriere della Sera* usually spoke for the average citizen of Milan. Even though the rich and famous were the ones photographed attending the opera, in Italy opera was beloved by everyone, not just the wealthy.

Taking Elle by the arm, he said to Jaime, "Enjoy!"

Elle smiled at the sight of Jaime sitting between two Italian beauties who were both obviously his dates. She supposed his ego was too big for just one woman tonight.

"Are you okay, sweetheart?" her mother asked, concerned, when they got to their table. "You've been gone for a while."

"Nerves," Elle said. "I'm not used to all of this." She and Dominic reclaimed their seats.

"Try to enjoy it," Natalie wisely told her. "After your performance tonight, it's your life from now on."

Dominic took Elle's hand and held on to it underneath the table.

"How did *you* handle the spotlight?" Elle asked Natalie.

"In my day the paparazzi were not as bad as they are today," Natalie told her. "We were granted some privacy." She smiled at Carlo sitting beside her. "Five years into my career I met Carlo, who was very supportive because my idol was his mother, Renata Corelli."

"She nearly fainted the first time she met my mother," Carlo said, lovingly gazing into his wife's eyes. "But Momma loved her on sight."

"Which made our marriage so much easier, in spite of the fact that most of his sisters *hated* me on sight," Natalie said with a laugh.

"But they changed their minds after they got to know her," Carlo informed Elle.

"Eventually," Natalie allowed. Elle smiled. Natalie was obviously still a little hurt by his sisters' rejection.

Natalie smiled at Elle. "Hopefully, you'll meet someone with whom you have a lot in common. There's nothing like that kind of support system." She gave her son a meaningful smile.

Dominic lowered his eyes and smiled. His mother didn't miss much. He looked across the table at Isobel Jones. She smiled at him in much the same way as his mother had. Oh, no, not both mothers! If they put their heads together and started matchmaking they would make his and Elle's life together a living hell. Perhaps it would be best to tell them he and Elle were dating. Then their mothers could transfer their considerable energies to some other area of their lives. Perhaps his imagination was running wild. He'd wait and see.

"Oh, that's not liable to happen anytime soon," Elle modestly said to Natalie's comment. "With my present schedule I would not even have time for a cup of coffee, let alone a romantic dinner."

"Sometimes the person who's right for you is already in your life," Natalie insisted. "Look around you. Isn't there someone who pays you a great deal of attention, someone you feel close to?" She leaned in. "Forgive me for repeating gossip but the word is Jaime Montoya has been very attentive to you."

"Jaime is very attentive to every beautiful woman who crosses his path," Dominic put in tightly. He instantly regretted his comment because his mother's and Isobel Jones's eyes were now riveted on him. *Jealous fool,* he chastised himself.

Then he saw something that was truly frightening:

his mother and Elle's mother gave each other smug looks as if he and Elle getting together was a done deal.

He glanced at Elle. She'd seen it, too.

They smiled at each other. "Let's tell them," he whispered.

"You do it," she whispered back.

He cleared his throat, getting the table's attention. Directing his words to his mother, he said, "I wanted you to get this gossip straight from the horse's mouth—Elle and I are dating."

Everyone started talking excitedly at once. Natalie stood up. "You let me drop all of those hints for nothing?"

"You seemed to be enjoying yourself," said Dominic, grinning.

He took Elle's hand and kissed it. Directing his next comment to Isobel, he said, "Don't worry, I intend to treat her like the queen she is."

"That would be appreciated," said Isobel, smiling warmly. Her eyes, however, were narrowed and in them Dominic saw the unspoken threat.

Natalie, still standing, raised her champagne glass. "A toast to the happy couple."

Dominic gazed into Elle's eyes as their glasses touched. He was truly happy. Everything was out in the open. They knew what to expect from each other. It was a match made in heaven.

Later, he watched as Elle hugged her mother and friends goodbye. They were going straight to the hotel to get some rest. They had an early flight tomorrow morning. He offered Elle his handkerchief as tears she couldn't hold back left tracks down her lovely face. She and her mother hugged a long time, parted and hugged again. Her friends Belana and Patrice each whispered something in her ear as they embraced her and gave him wary looks, as if they were not sure she should be left in his hands.

Only Erik Whitaker, Belana's brother, gave him a manly handshake and said with all sincerity, "You're a lucky guy. I've tried for years to get her to go out with me and she told me it would be like going out with her brother. More power to you!"

John Whitaker simply eyed him with a mixture of belligerence and resignation. "If you're her choice, then I hope you'll be happy together. Take care of her, she's special." Once again, he got the evil eye and the unspoken promise of bodily harm done to him if he didn't comply.

Dominic smiled reassuringly. "You don't have to worry."

Chapter 12

Once Dominic had Elle alone in his car he turned to her and asked, "How would you like to wake up in the most beautiful place on earth?"

"Are we going somewhere?" Elle asked eagerly.

"My villa on Lago di Como," he said as he started the car. It was after midnight and traffic was still moderately heavy, but he thought he could drive the twenty-five-plus miles to the villa in under an hour.

"I can pack in less than half an hour," Elle answered. She watched his profile. The beauty of the city lit up by glittering lights paled in comparison to him.

He smiled at her before returning his attention to the road. She reached over and gently rubbed his square jaw. "I didn't know you had a house on Lake Como."

"It was my grandmother's. She left it to me. I think you'll like it."

At her apartment, Dominic went upstairs with her

and kept kissing her, distracting her from the task at hand. Elle was trying to put clothes in a bag while he nibbled on her ear and kissed her on the neck. He couldn't keep his hands off her long enough for her to get anything done. After a few minutes of this, Elle gave up and turned into his arms for a lingering kiss. "Are we going to make love here or at Lake Como?" she asked when they came up for air. Her body was tingling all over. She wanted him now and was getting very impatient. She held his heated gaze with her fiery one. "What are you trying to do to me?" she asked breathlessly when he grabbed her behind and pulled her close.

He was so hard she was sure he was about to suggest they dispense with the packing and begin disrobing immediately. "I have everything set up at Lake Como," he finally admitted, looking sheepish.

Elle laughed. The great Dominic Corelli had staged her seduction just as he staged his operas. Planned down to the last detail!

"My God," she teased him lightly. "Make love to me already. You're driving me nuts!"

Dominic laughed, too. "You're pushy when you're horny."

"You haven't seen pushy yet," Elle warned him as she reached behind her and unzipped her dress. Seconds later she was standing in front of him in her bra and panties, which were satiny, a light gold shade and very sexy.

She watched the molten desire in his eyes turn into a covetous stare. *"Tesoro mio,"* he breathed as he reached out and pulled her against him. His lips caressed her warm body from neck to midriff. She moaned with pleasure. At last, he was touching her as she had only been able to dream about the past eight weeks.

Elle moaned with pleasure as his mouth covered hers in a deep, knee-weakening kiss. He broke off the kiss and took his hands off her long enough to quickly remove his suit. Elle helped as much as she could but only wound up getting frustrated with the buttons.

When he finally stood before her in his black boxer briefs, she felt somehow rewarded. "It's about time," she murmured, and they were kissing again.

Dominic picked her up, she wrapped her long legs around him, and he backed up until his muscular calves hit the bed. He fell backward onto the mattress with her on top.

Dominic rolled her over onto her back and gently unhooked the front-fastening bra.

Her full, heavy breasts spilled into his big hands and he bent and suckled, giving both nipples equal attention.

Elle writhed with pleasure beneath him. Her sex was wet and throbbing by this point and she was understandably ready for penetration, but Dominic by all appearances was having too good a time licking her all over.

He pulled down her panties and cupped her sex in his hand, reveling at the softness of the hair and the inviting warmth. He loved the smell of her so much he bent his head and tasted her. Elle tensed but Dominic gently kissed the inside of her thigh and she relaxed. He said something in soft Italian that she thought meant *elixir of the gods*. She spread her legs invitingly. Then his tongue plunged into her and she almost came then and there. But Dominic knew how to prolong her pleasure with his tongue and by the time he raised his head and smiled wickedly down at her, her legs felt like jelly and she was purring like a well-fed kitten.

He wasn't finished with her yet. Her body went through the rapturous throes of the most powerful orgasm she ever remembered having as his tongue did wonderful things to her. A muffled scream escaped and Dominic continued to give her pleasure.

Only after she stopped trembling did he get up and put on the condom that he took from his jacket pocket. Breathing hard, Elle watched him, his muscular golden-brown body moving with grace and power. His manhood was fully engorged and huge and her sex throbbed in anticipation of his entering her.

He straddled her and bent to kiss her mouth. The kiss deepened and Elle felt herself opening even further for him. Her body craved his completely and exultingly. She wrapped her arms around his neck as he entered her, and then she held on as he thrust slowly at first but more swiftly as he got into their rhythm. She couldn't believe it: he was bringing her to the point of release once again.

They were both breathing hard now and a thin layer of sweat had formed on their bodies. *Where has this man been all my life?* Elle thought as the second orgasm rocked her body. Then she moaned loudly and surrendered everything to him.

Dominic didn't want to come because if he did it would be over, this bliss, this wonderful sensation that had every nerve ending in his body in ecstasy. He just wanted to stay here within her, enjoying her: her silken skin, the play of muscles working against his own as they moved together, the scent of her skin, that spot just behind her ear that he had discovered made her quiver. He could stay like this forever, learning everything there was to know about her body.

Of course, man was not built for that, and one particularly sexy moan from her sent him over the edge and he came with a guttural growl. He fell on top of her and then rolled onto his side. They looked into each other's eyes and smiled, both instinctively knowing that something truly special had just happened between them.

"Do you still think singing is better than sex?" he asked teasingly.

Elle laughed softly. "Not by a long shot."

Elle wanted to say she loved him, but telling that to a man who didn't believe in love was not something a smart woman did. That would make him break the door down getting out of there.

Instead, she said, "So, what did I miss at Lake Como?"

"You missed a canopied bed with rose petals strewn across it, a scented bath with candles around the tub, good food and wine and Jeff Buckley singing 'Hallelujah' on the CD player."

"I love that song!" she said, her eyes devouring him.

He gently kissed the tip of her nose. "I thought you might."

"You planned a lovely evening," Elle told him.

"*Tesoro mio,* I already had everything I needed right here," Dominic told her. He looked at her with an intensity that made her toes curl. "You're so beautiful. More beautiful than anything I ever wrote. I'm humbled by your beauty."

"Flattery will get you everywhere," Elle said, and kissed him.

When they drew apart, Dominic smiled at her, hauled off and swatted her on the bottom. "Get up and get dressed. We're still going to Lake Como." He was getting up while he talked. "I want you to see the sunrise over the lake. I want to show you my favorite hiking trails."

Elle just lay there and smiled at him. "It's late, I want to sleep."

Dominic, however, was revitalized. "We're young and strong, we can sleep later. Come on, Jones, shake a leg!"

Elle shook a leg, literally. "But that's all that's shaking up in here." She yawned. "Your star is tired, Maestro. Please come back to bed and hold me until I fall asleep."

Dominic did come back to bed but it was only long enough to grab her and lift her up, sheet and all. When he began carrying her toward the bathroom with a mind to do some sort of mischief to her that Elle didn't want to imagine, she started wriggling and cried, "Okay, okay, I'll freshen up and put on my traveling clothes, Satan's spawn."

A few minutes later they were in the car heading north. "Lake Como is between the borders of Milan and Switzerland," he told her as he drove. "The villa is on the southern tip, so it's only about twenty-five miles away."

Elle yawned again. "This is all very interesting," she said. "Wake me when we get there." She curled up in her seat and was soon fast asleep, snoring softly.

Dominic smiled. He could get used to this.

* * *

Forty-five minutes later they were at his nineteenth-century villa on Lago di Como. Dominic got out of the car and went around to Elle's side. He opened her door. Elle turned her back on him, getting into a more comfortable sleeping position.

"Sleepyhead," Dominic called softly in an attempt to wake her.

"Go 'way," Elle mumbled.

Dominic reached in and gathered her up in his arms. While he was carrying her inside she snuggled closer, nuzzling his neck, her warm breath sending delicious shivers down his spine.

He didn't even have to open the door because Claudio, the elderly estate-keeper who lived here year-round, had heard the car approaching and knew it could only be the maestro. By the look of Claudio's huge eyes, though, he had not expected the maestro to bring a guest with him. Dominic didn't bring women to the villa. It was his spiritual retreat. It was the place where he went to unwind and get rid of the stresses of city life and work. He felt his grandmother's spirit here. And the last thing he wanted to do was disrespect his grandmother's memory with mistresses in the villa. Elle, though, was special. He believed his grandmother would have approved.

"*Buon giorno,*" Claudio said as he held the villa door wide for Dominic to enter.

"*Come stai,* Claudio?" Dominic said. "Did you get my message about the flowers and the wine and the other things I requested?"

"No," Claudio said, looking puzzled. "I'm afraid

I just got back tonight from visiting my sister in the hospital in Milan. I haven't checked the messages."

"Oh," Dominic said, concerned. "How is your sister?"

"She is doing much better, thank you," Claudio said as he smiled at the sleeping woman in Dominic's arms.

"This is Signorina Jones," Dominic told him. "She'll be our guest for the weekend."

Elle opened her eyes momentarily and smiled at Claudio. *"Buon giorno."*

"Benvenuto," Claudio said.

"Grazie," returned a still-drowsy Elle.

"Yes, all right," said Dominic. "We're going upstairs."

"Will you need anything else tonight, Maestro?" Claudio asked. He was a very short man in his sixties who had been an employee of Dominic's grandmother for many years, and when she died Dominic had kept him on to care for the villa. "No, Claudio. *Buona notte,*" Dominic said with a strained smile. It was a good thing he and Elle hadn't come earlier. None of his requests had been carried out.

He peered lovingly in her face as he carried her upstairs to his bed. As he entered the room he saw that Claudio continued to do an excellent job of maintaining the house. His bed had clean linen on it and it was already turned down.

He laid Elle on it and went back downstairs to get her bags. By the time he returned, Elle was hugging her pillow tightly, and her snoring seemed to have shifted into second gear. It was steady and not as loud; he supposed she was in REM sleep.

He put Elle's bags in the adjacent closet and came back out to coax her out of her jeans, shirt and athletic shoes. She was sleepily cooperative.

When he was down to her bra and panties he debated whether or not to remove them. He decided not to. If she should awaken in the middle of the night and choose to take them off that was another thing, but he didn't want her thinking that something had happened between them while she was asleep. He was a gentleman, after all.

He stripped down to his briefs and got into bed next to Elle. She naturally snuggled close to him, throwing her arm across his chest and digging her nose into his shoulder. Dominic smiled as he turned out the light on the nightstand. Moonlight spilled in through sheer curtains at the balcony doors. There would be a full moon tomorrow night. He planned to take Elle for a boat ride so they could watch the moonbeams dance on the water and maybe get into some mischief themselves.

Elle moaned in her sleep. "Dominic," she said sultrily.

He kissed her forehead. She'd finally called him Dominic! Not Signor Corelli, or Maestro, or the devil incarnate or Satan's spawn. Dominic. He closed his eyes and sleep claimed him shortly afterward.

Elle awoke in the middle of the night and was momentarily disoriented. The events of the night then quickly came to mind. She was lying on her side with her leg thrown across Dominic's muscular thighs. Her face was inches from his shoulder. He was sleeping soundly and she didn't want to wake him, but she suddenly got a strong urge to go to the bathroom.

She slowly inched her way to the opposite side of the bed and got out using as few movements as possible. Still, Dominic woke up. Not with a start as she might when awakened, but alert. He reached over and switched on the bedside lamp. "Through there," he said, pointing in the direction of the bathroom.

Elle felt somewhat embarrassed. This was, after all, the first time she had ever gone to the bathroom when he was in the room and could possibly hear her tinkle. "Thanks," she said and hurried to the bathroom, where she quietly closed the door behind her and sat on the toilet. It was a large room with a walk-in shower on one side and a sunken tub on the other. Must be nice to have a choice, she thought lightly as she peed as quietly as possible.

Finished, she got up and freshened herself with a moist personal wipe from the pop-up dispenser on the long double sink. She wondered if this bedroom suite had been used by Dominic's grandmother and her husband. Two sinks. She could see why a woman would want her own sink, since some men left hairs and God-knows-what-else on theirs after using it.

Dominic knocked on the door. "Did I hear you flush? I've got to go, too."

Elle quickly deposited the used wipe in the trash, pulled up her panties and washed her hands. She opened the door and smiled at Dominic. "It's all yours."

He quickly entered, pulled down the front of his briefs and didn't wait for her to leave.

Okay, thought Elle, *that was a little too familiar for me.* She shut the door. It was not something she wanted to witness, no matter how many years they were together.

She laughed softly as she got back into bed. Where had that thought come from? She and Dominic were not going to be together that long. He'd made it clear that there was no real future for them. They were living for the here and now. They were a sophisticated, twenty-first-century couple. There were no rules for them. They made them up as they went along.

She sighed as she punched her pillow and laid her head on it. Whom was she fooling? What did she know about the rules of romance?

When it came to sexual experience she was sorely lacking. Two partners, including Dominic, and the first one had cheated on her so she couldn't have been that exciting in bed. Although…to be fair…making love to Dominic had been a whole lot different from making love to Tony. Tony was interested in getting in and getting off. Dominic was interested in making sure she enjoyed herself as much as he did. And, she had to admit, she had given as good as she had gotten.

She smiled again, this time with cunning satisfaction. So what if there was no possibility of love for this relationship? She was a woman now and every woman should be able to look back and say she had at least one good lover in her lifetime. Dominic Corelli would be hers. This was their love affair. She was going to enjoy it.

Dominic came back to the bedroom wearing nothing but a smile. Elle blushed when she lowered her eyes to his semi-erect manhood, but she didn't look away.

Unashamed, he stood and let her get an eyeful. "I usually sleep in the nude. That won't bother you, will it? I know how fond you are of pajamas."

Elle laughed shortly. "No, I like you naked."

He came and sat beside her. "I left your underwear on you when I put you to bed," he told her. "But if you want to change into something more comfortable now, your bags are in the closet."

Elle did. Sleeping in a bra always felt constrictive to her so she got up and went looking for something to sleep in. Besides pajamas, she'd packed a rather sexy silken red nightgown. She put that on and returned to the bedroom.

After she got back into bed Dominic reached for her. She settled close to his side with her head in the crook of his arm. He turned down the light but didn't turn it off completely. "This is a huge room," Elle said. "How big *is* this villa?"

"It has six bedrooms," Dominic told her. "My grandparents had a big family. They lived in Milan but this was their vacation home. When my parents married, my grandmother gave the Milan house to them as a wedding present. Her daughters all made good marriages and had husbands who built them homes. She wanted the house to remain in the family. Dad took over the family business after Grandpa died, and for a while my grandmother lived with my parents. But, later, she wanted solitude so she moved here year-round. I visited her often and came to love this place. She knew how I felt about it so she left it to me."

"How often do you come here?"

"Only on weekends, and for the month of August when Milanese who can afford it vacation on the lake to avoid the heat of the city. Claudio takes care of it in my absence."

"Who's Claudio?"

He laughed softly. "Oh, yeah, you were pretty drowsy

through the introductions. He's the caretaker. He has a habit of staying scarce unless you call him, but you'll probably run into him once or twice while you're here. He lives in a cottage on the grounds. Don't be surprised if you see a funny-looking little fellow with snow-white hair around the villa."

"Okay," said Elle, her tone sexy.

She ran her hand over his chest. He was hairy but not excessively so. The hair was curly and soft. Going lower, she could feel the muscles in his six-pack. For abdominals like that, she knew he had to work out religiously. Dominic Corelli was disciplined, of that she was well aware. He'd worked them hard during rehearsals, never settling for anything less than what he considered perfection.

Elle's hand stopped moving.

Dominic tensed. He had been anticipating her hand going down farther and grasping his member. "What's wrong?" he asked huskily.

"You're perfect," Elle said forlornly.

She sat up in bed and propped her pillows behind her. Feeling at a disadvantage lying down, Dominic did the same. "I'm glad you think so, but what has that got to do with anything?" he asked.

"I don't know if you've noticed but I've got curves," Elle said. "I'm not fat, but I'll never be as skinny as some of the women I see walking around Milan."

"You mean fashion models?" asked Dominic, laughter evident in his tone. "They're clothes hangers, Elle. Their bodies don't mirror the bodies of most women in the world."

"Then you like a woman with curves," Elle said hopefully.

"Listen, Elle," Dominic told her, looking her straight in the eyes. "I love your body. You're strong and you're soft at the same time. I especially like your ass. It's perfectly shaped and gives me something wonderful to hold on to. I can think about your ass and get hard. I know. I've done it."

"Whoa," Elle said, laughing softly. "Dominic Corelli, an ass man? I'd never have thought it."

Dominic grabbed her around the waist and pulled her down onto her side. They kissed and Elle forgot all about what she perceived as her little imperfections.

Dominic began pulling at the waistband of her panties and she twisted and wriggled until he managed to get them past her hips. Then it was easy to pull them off and toss them aside. Next he pulled the nightgown over her head and threw it onto the end of the bed. For as long as it had been on her body, Elle could have saved time by never putting it on at all.

Now there was nothing between them. Warm skin slid against warm skin. Her sex welcomed the feel of his hardened penis rubbing against it. She imagined her sex was her mouth and her lips would open and welcome him inside. This fantasy only made her sex throb with want of release even more.

Dominic felt her urgent need and hurriedly reached over and got a condom off the nightstand. Elle didn't have the patience to wait for him to put it on, so she snatched it from him and rolled it onto his long, thick, hard member herself.

Dominic lay on his back and pulled her on top of him. "Get your pleasure," he said. "I want to watch you."

Straddling him, Elle positioned him at the opening

of her sex, and while his big hands caressed her breasts, gently rubbing her nipples until they were hard, highly sensitive nubs, she pushed until he was fully inside of her. Then she rode him until they were both writhing with pent-up passion, but she withheld their release. She stopped and bent to kiss him deeply, enjoying the taste of his mouth, relishing the masterful thrusts of his tongue against hers. She squeezed the muscles of her vagina to grab his penis, holding it and then slowly letting it go. Dominic sighed. She felt so good to him.

Then, he was bucking beneath her because he couldn't hold off any longer. With each thrust, he pushed against Elle's clitoris and she came with a shout, her vaginal muscles quivering as the orgasm hit her in waves. Dominic stiffened as an orgasm rocked him almost simultaneously.

Elle collapsed on top of him. He felt her vaginal walls quivering with release. She felt his penis throbbing like a heartbeat. Kissing his mouth gently, she said, "Bravo, Maestro."

Dominic smiled. *"Grazie, cara mia."*

Chapter 13

When Elle awakened it was morning. Golden sunlight shone through the sheers at the doors and through them she could see the silhouette of a man standing on the balcony.

She took stock of herself. Still naked, *yes;* morning breath, *probably;* need to freshen up before greeting your lover, *definitely.* She got out of bed and hurried into the bathroom. Then came right back out because it occurred to her that she was going to need her toothbrush.

She went into the huge closet and grabbed one of her bags. Toiletries in hand, she rushed back through the bedroom and had almost reached the bathroom when she heard the balcony doors creak open. She froze.

"Oh, Elle, you're up," Dominic said, smiling. He was freshly showered and dressed in jeans and a cotton crewneck sweater in royal blue. He looked like a preppie.

"Pretend you don't see me," Elle said and continued to the bathroom.

"But I do see you and I want my morning kiss," Dominic said, grinning mischievously as he quickly crossed the room.

Elle dashed to the bathroom and closed and locked the door.

Dominic went to the door and called, "Is this another one of your pet peeves? No kisses before you brush? Because I think I should be making a list or something."

"I see you're looking rather refreshed," Elle lightly accused.

"Guilty as charged," Dominic answered. "I showered in one of the other bathrooms so I wouldn't disturb your beauty sleep."

"You're very considerate," said Elle. "Now go away so I can shower and do whatever other mysterious things I have to do in the morning in order to look less like Quasimodo."

Laughing, Dominic said, "All right, *cara mia.* I'll go make breakfast."

"Okay!" Elle called, relieved.

Standing in front of the mirror, she assessed her hair. She'd forgotten her shower cap! She waited until she thought she heard the bedroom door shut before she opened the bathroom door and went back into the bedroom. But Dominic had hidden behind the bathroom door and grabbed Elle and kissed her before she had the chance to protest.

Elle pushed his chest with both hands, trying to gain

enough purchase to shove him away. But he didn't let her go until he was good and ready.

"There," he said, releasing her. "Your theory is proven wrong. Your morning breath didn't disgust me." His gaze traveled the length of her body. "In fact, I'm all for going back to bed."

Elle saw the bulge in his jeans. "I can see that," she said. "But the answer is no, Satan's spawn. I'm going to shower just like you did and brush my teeth. Love the taste of your toothpaste, by the way. Minty fresh!" And with that, she returned to the bathroom and locked him out.

Dominic went to the door. "Are you always this cranky in the morning?"

"Not after my first cup of coffee," Elle told him. "Now, be a good boy and leave me alone!"

Laughing, Dominic left her in peace.

Looking at her reflection in the bathroom mirror, Elle scowled. She still hadn't gotten the shower cap. Damn that Dominic Corelli! She smiled suddenly. That kiss had been something else.

Her cell phone was ringing when she came out of the bathroom later, wrapped in a towel. She dug the phone out of her purse and carefully read the name and number on its screen: her mother's.

She quickly answered. "Isobel, where are you?"

"We're in Switzerland. Apparently, John has business here. We'll be spending the night."

"You mean he didn't tell you his itinerary before he asked you to join them on his jet?"

"Not a word," Isobel said, sounding miffed.

"My mother the jet-setter," Elle said, laughing. "You

don't have to be back at work until Monday. Try to enjoy yourself."

"That's the problem, I am!" cried Isobel.

"Why is it a problem?"

Isobel paused for what seemed like a long time to Elle, but in actuality was only a few seconds. "Because I think he wants to ask me out but hasn't gotten up the nerve. I can feel it." She stopped again. Elle was beginning to wonder if maybe she was pausing for so long because she didn't want someone nearby to overhear her conversation.

"You're not alone?"

"Yeah, I'm alone, I'm just upset."

"Because you suspect he wants to get to know you better?"

"He scares me, Elle!"

"John Whitaker?" Elle said, incredulous. "He's a sweetheart."

"Yes, it would seem so. To the untrained eye he looks like a successful businessman who's managed to stay on top by outmaneuvering his competition. That's an awesome quality in this day and age. What's more, he seems to have done it without being ruthless. Plus in a time of government bailouts, his company is going strong and his employees love him. Talk about a miracle worker!"

Elle laughed softly. "Sounds like you like him."

"I can't deny that I admire him," said Isobel.

"Then what's the problem?" Elle wanted to know.

"He's almost as rich as Gates," Isobel answered. "I'd never be comfortable in the circles he runs in, Elle. We're so unsuitable for one another."

Elle sighed. Hadn't she thought the same thing about

herself and Dominic? She still wasn't that confident of being capable of keeping up with him. But she knew two things—she was as smart as he was, even if she didn't have his money, and she was willing to take risks.

"Every relationship is a risk," she told her mother. "I can feel you coming out of your shell, Isobel Jones. It's time. Whether it's with the stockbroker or John Whitaker, financial giant, it's time you took a leap of faith and got back out there. You're in your prime, for God's sake. Haven't you missed having a good man in your life?"

Elle knew her mother had casually dated over the years, but when a guy started to talk about getting serious she would make an excuse and break up with him. It was as if she was doing it first, before he could dump her.

"I see so many women who're alone, whether it's through divorce, death or abandonment," Isobel said. "Some of my friends are in their early fifties, and they've never been married. They're not sad about it, either. They own their homes. Have savings in the bank. Are doing it for themselves, as that Aretha song goes. I don't need a man in my life, Elle."

"Especially not one who might hurt you," Elle said intuitively.

"I'm not as young as you are. I might not bounce back," Isobel said in warning tones. It was as if she were asking her daughter for permission to go ahead and let herself be wined and dined by John Whitaker, if he was so inclined.

"I say, go for it," Elle said with a determined note in her voice.

Isobel laughed. "Why am I panicking? He hasn't so much as asked me out for a cup of coffee!"

"He's had his eye on you for some time now," Elle frankly told her. "I couldn't help noticing you two at the opening last night. He was giving you a lot of admiring glances. You didn't seem to mind the attention."

"What woman wouldn't be flattered?" Isobel asked a bit breathlessly.

"Elle, breakfast is ready!" she suddenly heard Dominic yell from downstairs.

"Is that Dominic I hear in the background?" her mother asked.

Darn these high-sound-quality cell phones, Elle silently groused. "Ah...yeah," she said, deciding it was best not to lie to her mother. "We're at his house on the lake. It's in a little town not far from Milan. We drove here shortly after we said goodbye to you all." Elle waited for her mother's reaction.

"You know what you want out of life," Isobel said after a long pause. "I'm not going to give you dire warnings about the consequences of trusting the wrong man with your body. You know what they are. Just take care of yourself, baby."

"I will, Ma," Elle promised.

Isobel sniffed. Elle was well aware that her mother had started crying as soon as she had heard that her daughter was in a love nest with a man she'd only known for two months, and not because Elle had called her Ma.

"I wish I were there to hug you."

Elle moaned loudly as if she were hugging her mother. "Consider yourself hugged."

Isobel moaned back. "All right," she said after she'd

stopped. "Goodbye, baby, and tell Dominic I said hello."

"I will. Goodbye," Elle said fondly.

She put the phone down and went to the closet for clothes similar to Dominic's, jeans and a shirt. By the time she got downstairs he had set the table on the patio and was dishing up eggs scrambled with red peppers and chives, and savory Italian breakfast sausage. Fresh bread, butter and jam were on the table, too, along with a carafe of freshly brewed coffee.

She had taken the time to admire the house en route to the kitchen. It reminded her of the villa in the film *Enchanted April*, furnished with antiques. It had beautiful marble floors, airy high ceilings and French doors all around that opened outside to fragrant flower gardens that were lush and green. It apparently received a lot of tender loving care.

Claudio must be a very good caretaker. Houses this size needed constant repairs and touch-ups. She ought to know: the brownstone where she grew up was always in need of fresh paint, a new this or a new that.

"There you are!" Dominic said when she entered the kitchen. He removed his apron, tossed it onto a nearby chair and went and hugged her.

Elle closed her eyes and enjoyed it. He smelled good, and he felt good, with his firm body pressed close to her soft curves. She shyly kissed the side of his neck, then stuck her nose in that spot and inhaled his heady body odor, a combination of soap and his own unique male scent.

"You smell good enough to eat," she told him.

"Maybe later," he said with a wicked glint in his eye.

Elle laughed and kissed him. This kiss was as intense

as the one they'd shared upstairs, if somewhat longer. Elle was breathless when he set her down. *Down* being the operative word, because he had lifted her off the floor sometime during the kiss, and she was so into the kiss she hadn't even noticed.

She sighed contentedly, "A girl could get used to that."

"So could a boy," Dominic said, holding the patio door open for her. "Your repast awaits, *cara mia.*"

He and Elle ate like kings, as they relived the events of last night. Dominic explained that a good opening night usually meant a nice, long run for the opera.

Later, they went for a walk in the woods. Elle loved the outdoors and was delighted by the different indigenous trees, flowers and shrubs, which he knew by name. He picked wildflowers for her and presented her with a beautiful bouquet.

It was midday when they arrived at a grassy knoll overlooking the lake. Dominic took off the backpack he'd been carrying and began removing items from it. First he spread a blanket on the grass and then he took out a chilled bottle of wine and two wineglasses enveloped in Bubble Wrap. Elle marveled at his attention to detail. She wondered when he had had the time to do it all.

Dominic looked up at the sky, his grin wide. "It's a beautiful day, eh?"

"Just perfect," Elle agreed dreamily, her eyes on him.

He handed Elle a glass of Chianti and she sniffed it and swirled it around in the glass. After he poured his he did the same, then touched the rim of his glass to hers. "To many idyllic days like this," he intoned. His soulful brown eyes held her gaze. Elle took a sip. It had a delicious, fruity, refreshing quality.

Dominic handed her half a roast beef sandwich on thick homemade bread with spicy brown mustard. He kept the other half.

They enjoyed it in silence as they watched boats on the lake drift by. "No speedboats today," Dominic commented after a while. "I hate them. They upset the tranquility of the setting."

Elle changed position, putting her long legs out in front of her. He was right, this was a peaceful spot. She could lie back and fall asleep right here and sleep the afternoon away. She sighed. She must really be tired after those grueling rehearsals to be thinking of napping when she had an Italian lover only two feet away.

She gave him a quizzical look. "Have you always loved peace and quiet?"

Dominic smiled at her. "No, I was a wild child in my youth."

Elle laughed at him. "In your youth," she said derisively. "You're only thirty-three."

"Well, in my teens," Dominic said. "I drove too fast, got drunk, had sex with any willing girl. I put my parents through hell."

Elle was truly surprised by his admission. "I imagined that you have always been disciplined, and hard on yourself, the way you are today," she told him.

"No, I had my rebellious stage," Dominic told her. He smiled, remembering. "You see, my father started grooming me to take over the family business as soon as I came out of my mother's womb, if not sooner." He laughed shortly. "I wouldn't be surprised if he told me he used to talk to me about the business while I was still in her belly. He told me that, from the moment Momma told him she was carrying me, he knew that I was a boy and would be the next Corelli to head the company. Imagine his disappointment when from the time I was three I demonstrated a talent for music. I was like you—I could hear a tune and play it by ear. Papa was devastated. My mother and my grandmother said it was a gift from God. Papa thought it must be from Satan. If I pursued music, where would that leave him? He had an obsessive fear that when the time came there would be no one to inherit the family business. When my mother was pregnant with Sophia and Ana, I prayed that they would be boys. I believe that from an early age Sophia resented my father for not considering his daughters likely candidates to take over the business. But he stuck to his belief that I was just going through a phase and I would give up music."

Riveted, Elle asked, "What happened to make him realize it wasn't a phase?"

"I entered a young composers contest given by La Scala and won," he said. "I was fifteen. I was given a full music scholarship. I was sent to a boarding school that specialized in preparing young people for careers in music."

"Like Juilliard," Elle said softly.

"Yes, except it was in Switzerland," Dominic told her.

"I remember reading about that. How long did you go to school there?"

"From fifteen till twenty-one," he answered, his smile gone.

Sensing something bad had happened to him at that school in Switzerland, Elle reached over and grasped his free hand in hers.

"I'm listening," she gently said.

She set her sandwich down on its wax paper wrapping and reached for his other hand. He gave it to her and, after taking a deep breath, continued. "In a last-ditch effort to conform me to his ways, my dad took me out of school when I turned twenty-one. 'You're a man now,' he said. 'You can't continue to have pipe dreams. It's time to face reality—you are my heir. You must learn the business.'"

"How did you handle it?" Elle asked, brows knitted in a deep frown.

"I went out partying with the first lowlifes I could find. I didn't have any friends here. All of my friends were at school in Switzerland. We got drunk, trashed a bar, you can't imagine what stupid things you think of doing when you believe your life is no longer in your control and nothing matters. Add alcohol to the equation and you have a recipe for disaster. The elderly man who owned the bar got hurt during the scuffle. He wound up in the hospital with a concussion and we ended up in jail. It was the single most stupid thing I've ever done in my life."

"So your trip to headquarters to rescue me wasn't the first time you'd been in a police station."

He smiled again. "No. It was the most humiliating night of my life. My mother and father had to come down and bail me out. That was the first time I met Felix Filianoti, the lawyer who helped you that night."

"Yes, I'm grateful to him," Elle said.

"Felix pleaded my case, explaining that I had never been in trouble before, and assured them I would never do anything so foolish again. My father, he said, was a fine, upstanding businessman and my mother was the great Natalie Davis who had sung at La Scala. I believe that impressed them more than my father's credentials." He paused. "On the way home in the car my father told me I was free. 'Free?' I asked. 'Free from what?'

"'Free to pursue your music,' he told me. 'If being denied your calling is going to turn you into a criminal, then I set you free.'"

He smiled at Elle. "There were no hard feelings between us. He loved me just as much as he had always loved me, and I loved him more. I was free to be me."

"You finished your first opera when you were twenty-three," Elle said in an awe-filled voice. "That's amazing."

"Not really," Dominic said. "I started it when I was sixteen. It took me seven years to finish it."

"But it was worth it," Elle said. "*Inferno* has been performed all over the world. Music from it has been used in major films, and artists from opera and pop music have covered the songs. It's a wonderful piece of work."

He held her gaze. "How do you know that opera so well? You sang the opening aria at your audition and then you played 'Burn in Hell' as if you'd written it."

"*Inferno* was our senior class project," Elle told him. "Every year an opera was chosen and the senior class performed the starring roles. I had the lead soprano part, so I must have sung that aria a hundred times.

It's embedded in my memory. And because I love your music, I learned the entire score my senior year."

"I'm impressed," Dominic said with sincerity. "Tell me more about you. Where did you get your voice?"

Elle felt her tear ducts filling up. Every time she thought of her grandfather and hearing his glorious voice on Sunday morning, she wanted to cry. "I know you've heard of Paul Robeson," she said.

"The black social activist, singer and actor from the early twentieth century," Dominic said.

"I've never quite heard him described that way," Elle said.

"I'm sorry, but I learned about him from a history book," Dominic explained.

"No, you're exactly right," Elle said. "It's just that when I was growing up I always heard him described in glowing terms. My grandfather and his contemporaries adored Paul Robeson. They would listen to his recordings endlessly. And my grandfather's bass voice was so close to his that it was almost impossible to tell them apart. That's where I get my voice, from my grandfather. He was also the first person to tell me I was talented. He played piano, too, and we would spend hours at the piano, singing together. I think my range is the way it is today because I used to try to mimic his bass voice."

Dominic nodded, understanding completely. "Yes, in your lower registers you have a purity that astounds me. You know, you're probably not a mezzo-soprano at all. You're probably a contralto, but you sing mezzo-soprano very well."

"What are you?" Elle asked.

Dominic smiled and picked up his sandwich. "I told you, I don't sing."

"You're lying," Elle said with certainty, her eyes filled with humor. "Your speaking voice alone sends chills down my spine. You're either a baritone or a tenor. One of these days, you're going to sing for me."

"Don't hold your breath, my darling girl," Dominic said. "Eat your sandwich. You're going to need your strength later."

Elle eyed him curiously. "For what, exactly?" she asked.

"Tonight, I'm going to take you out in my boat and make love to you under the light of the full moon," Dominic promised.

Elle blushed and picked up her sandwich. "Well, I guess I do need my strength."

They ate in silence from that point on, stealing steamy glances at one another and smiling. They were happy, truly happy, just being together.

Chapter 14

"It's back to work tomorrow," Dominic said wistfully. It was a little after nine in the evening and he and Elle had just had dinner together on the deck of his forty-five-foot sailboat. The sails were lowered and the anchor was down so the only motion was a gentle rocking caused by the wind and the lake's currents.

They were lounging on the long, padded seating area on the foredeck. Dominic was sitting with his arms around Elle, legs stretched out, his back supported, and Elle was sitting between his legs, her back against his chest, her legs also outstretched.

Both were casually dressed in jeans, shirts and deck shoes. Because the air was cool, and when the breezes blew it was cold, they were sharing a blanket. They were also sharing a bottle of wine, which was almost gone. The mood was mellow.

"So, there are going to be two or three days

separating each performance," Elle said. She'd gone over the schedule earlier.

"Yes, to give the singers time to rest their voices. This way we get the optimal performance out of them," Dominic said. "Teatro alla Scala has to be able to justify their high ticket prices."

Elle laughed softly. "Everybody complains about it. But, really, when you buy a ticket aren't you also paying for the ambience, the reputation and the historical significance of the theater?"

"You should give that one to the theater's publicity department. It would sell even more tickets," Dominic joked.

"I'm just saying that when you go to La Scala you're going there for the whole experience, not just for the opera or the ballet or some other entertainment event that you're going to see."

"Yes, dear, but ultimately you go there for the superior entertainment," Dominic insisted.

"I'm not arguing the point," Elle said. "But when I think of La Scala I think of all the wonderful singers who've performed there, like Pavarotti, Grace Bumbry, Maria Callas, Denyce Graves, Leontyne Price. It has an enviable history of great performances. To say nothing of the composers who debuted their operas at La Scala. All the *i*'s."

"The eyes?" Dominic asked, puzzled.

"The alphabet, *i,*" Elle said. "Verdi, Rossini, Puccini."

Dominic laughed. "Corelli."

"My favorite *i,*" Elle said, twisting her torso around to kiss his lips.

As the kiss deepened, she got up on her knees to get in a more comfortable position.

Dominic was delighted. He liked it when she desired him. The Latin lover in him wouldn't let him be subjugated in lovemaking, but it was nice to know she wanted him as much as he wanted her.

He had to stop her now, though, because although the cushion beneath them was soft, the bench was far too narrow to make love on. So he gently broke off the kiss, got up, took her by the hand and led her below, the wine and glasses abandoned on the deck and the blanket in Elle's hand trailing after her.

In the well-appointed cabin, Elle tossed the blanket onto the big bed and began to slowly and methodically peel off her clothes. Dominic alternated between watching her and taking his eyes off her long enough to walk over to the CD player and switch it on.

Aretha's voice filled the space as she sang, "You're a liar and you're a cheat, and I don't know why I let you do these things to me...."

Dominic began pulling off his clothes, too, his body swaying to the music. Elle watched. He had good moves, sexy and assured. He pulled the shirt he was wearing open to reveal his muscular chest and stomach. Elle sighed, remembered she was also getting undressed and resumed.

Above them the moon was full and its bright light shone down on them through the skylight. It was the only illumination in the cabin and cast a pale white light on their brown bodies. The effect was almost ethereal to Elle, like a dream she'd recently had about them—a very sensual dream.

Nude, they met in the middle of the cabin and embraced.

"Cara mia," Dominic breathed, his hands caressing her shoulders, moving down to her back and then her bottom. "I don't think I'll ever get enough of you."

He honestly felt that way. Of the lovers he'd had he could not recall any who had made him feel this way. It was like a hunger that he thought had been sated the last time he'd had his fill, only to realize later that he was even more ravenous. The feeling increased exponentially until he felt he would go crazy if he didn't touch her. Like now, his excitement was such that he didn't know where to touch her or kiss her first: Her neck, her breasts, that spot he liked behind her ear? It was all sweet to him.

After months and months of deprivation, having no one touch her intimately at all, Elle's body was practically singing with joy! That sensation was magnified by the fact that she loved him. It was a doomed love, but love nonetheless.

She would stay as long as it lasted.

Dominic picked her up and put her down on the bed. Elle pulled him on top of her, opened her legs and welcomed him inside of her. Their loving was fierce and near violent, as if passion had possessed them and their actions were not their own, and therefore couldn't be reined in.

Their kisses were hungry and designed to pull as much succor from each other as possible. It was an intimate urgency that was totally out of control.

Everything she couldn't say to him was expressed in her lovemaking.

After several minutes of this sensual intensity Elle's

body stiffened and she arched her back. She moaned loudly and scratched his sides as the orgasm rocked her. Dominic went deeper and enjoyed the feel of the multiple contractions she was having.

It was only when he was about to ejaculate inside of her that Dominic's feverish mind suddenly realized that he wasn't wearing a condom. But she felt so good to him that he debated whether or not it was worth the risk. At the last moment he pulled out and hoped irrationally that, since he was a Catholic, the rhythm method could somehow magically work for him. Or Elle could be on the pill. That would be a godsend.

His seed spilled onto her belly and he collapsed on top of her, but quickly removed his weight from her body and lay beside her.

Elle, breathing hard, noticed the wetness, which seemed like a lot more than she was used to, and put her hand on her belly. She instantly knew what the thick dampness was and tried not to panic. She sat up. "The condom broke?" she asked, keeping her tone as normal as she could manage at that moment.

"No, I forgot the condom," Dominic admitted. "But I pulled out before I ejaculated. Don't worry, I've been tested. I'm healthy."

Elle hadn't thought that he might be HIV positive. But she knew that in this day and age, it should have at least been somewhere in the back of her mind to find out. Talk about being blinded by lust!

But HIV was not her only immediate concern. "I'm not on the pill, Dominic. Although I'm healthy, too, we can never forget the condom!"

Dominic sat on the side of bed and held his head

in his hands. "We should have talked about this before...."

Elle sighed. "Okay, well now we know. I'm not getting on the pill because it messes with my hormones, so that's not a solution for birth control with us. We've got to rely on condoms unless you want to..."

The word *vasectomy* flashed in Dominic's mind and he cried, "No, I'm not letting a doctor near me."

Elle smiled. "But you don't want children. It would be the perfect solution."

"It's not going to happen, Elle, so get off the subject!" Dominic said loudly.

Elle laughed. "Calm down, I was only pulling your leg. I would never ask you to do that. I expect you to respect my wishes about not taking the pill."

Dominic laughed softly. "All right, I won't forget the condoms again."

Elle reached up and patted his strong jaw. "Good." She climbed out of bed. "I'm going to freshen up."

Dominic watched her go, his desire for her still high even after what had just happened between them. So, now he knew there was a risk of pregnancy if they weren't careful. Strangely enough, that didn't send him into a panic. Worse things could happen than having a child with a woman like Elle.

By the time Dominic pulled the boat into the dock adjacent to the villa, it was late. After making love they had unfurled the sails, raised the anchor and toured the lake district. They called hello to fellow night boaters and drank in the beauty of the romantic landscape, of the villas lit up and sitting high on hills, to say nothing of the moon.

While they sailed they talked about everything under

the sun, from world politics to religion, and Dominic finally revealed why the devil figured prominently in all of his operas. "I'm not saying that I prefer him over God, but I can certainly understand his point of view," he began. "He was one of God's favorite angels. He was assigned the task of watching over humans and he began to covet their adoration, so he took it upon himself to get them to worship him. The only way for that to happen was to get them thrown out of the Garden of Eden. Then they would have to depend on him. Unfortunately for him, his plans didn't work out—he wound up getting tossed out of heaven, and Adam and Eve got tossed out of paradise. All because he disobeyed his father by wanting to go out on his own."

Elle thought she could see where this was going, and said, "You're saying that because you didn't want to follow in your father's footsteps, you were demonized by him?"

"Made to feel unworthy," Dominic said, surprised that she had put two and two together so quickly. "It wasn't intentional, of course, but that was the end result."

"And because Satan disobeyed God by wanting Adam and Eve to worship him, he was demonized," Elle said. "You know, I've read my Bible, too. My grandfather made sure of that. Before the war in heaven between Satan and his followers who were rebellious angels and the archangel Michael and his faithful angels, there was no such thing as a demon. The losers, those rebellious angels who followed Satan, were tossed out of heaven and after that were known as demons."

Dominic was nodding as he steered the boat toward the villa's dock. "That's right."

"So you identify with Satan because you were a rebellious son, too."

"Yes," said Dominic, smiling. "That doesn't mean I want to worship him or anything. It just means I find his situation fascinating. I wonder if he's doomed forever, or if God will give him a chance to redeem himself in the end?"

"And that's why you give him human qualities in your operas. You make him fall in love to see if he has the capacity to love."

Dominic maneuvered the sailboat into its slip. Then all was silent around them except for the lapping of water against the boat's sides. "I know it's silly," he said, "a being like Satan falling in love. But it's very dramatic, isn't it, the notion of the embodiment of evil falling in love with a human? Then again, it's not such a far stretch of the imagination, since Satan has been observing humans for aeons. Why shouldn't he have developed affection for them?"

Elle laughed. "Because he's the embodiment of evil!" she cried. He laughed, too.

Together, they secured the boat. As they walked up the hill to the villa hand in hand Dominic said to her, "You're the only person I ever told that. I wonder why?" He looked at her with an enigmatic smile.

Elle smiled back. "Maybe because you knew I wouldn't laugh at you."

"But you did laugh," he reminded her.

"Yes, but I laughed *with* you, not at you."

The next three months passed quickly. Elle's life was consumed by work: going to rehearsals, appearing nearly nightly in the opera and practicing drills with her voice coach. On weekends she and Dominic went to the villa.

The opera did so well that Dominic started getting offers from other opera houses around the world that wanted to produce it in their venues even before it ran its course in Milan.

Three weekends out of those three months were devoted to recording the cast album of *Temptation*. All of these developments were exciting for Elle. Her energy never seemed to lag. It was as if she were being carried on a wave of new and wondrous things. Opera houses in London, Madrid, Munich, Paris and New York wanted her to star in their productions of *Temptation*. Her new agent, Blanca Mendes, was calling her nearly every day with more news.

After the play closed in Milan she and Dominic went to the villa and stayed there for a month. Dominic was working on a new opera and Elle got the chance to hear his piano playing well into the night. When he was creating he was very nearly a madman and she could see that he was one of those artists who suffered through the process.

She, on the other hand, believed that art could be conceived in joy.

They had been at the villa for two weeks when Elle, unable to sleep due to Dominic's impassioned playing, got up and went downstairs to the music room.

He was so involved with his music that he didn't notice he had an audience. Elle stood outlined in the doorway wearing a short, sheer white sleeveless nightgown. His playing touched her. This opera was different from his other three. It didn't involve spiritual beings like the devil and angels. It was about a human who had been bitten and had to live his life as a vampire. For over two centuries he had roamed the earth, his life one of solitude because he couldn't get close to anyone for fear of them learning his identity. Then, he meets a very special woman who accidentally finds out he's immortal. She is not repulsed by it but is fascinated, and they fall in love. She asks him to turn her into a vampire. But can he do that to the woman he loves? He has suffered greatly. She argues that if she is turned, then he will never have to be alone again. It's very tempting. In the end, though, he can't do it and falls on his own sword, ending his suffering and giving her the chance to live a normal life. Elle loved the story, loosely based on Bram Stoker's *Dracula*.

She was standing in the doorway listening to the man she loved create a work of art, when Dominic abruptly stopped playing, startling Elle. He rose. "How long have you been there?" he asked, his tone gentle, not in the least accusing.

Elle began walking toward him. The marble floor was cool beneath her bare feet. She liked the feel, though. Since she'd been with Dominic she had discovered a sensual side to her personality. Pleasure for her didn't begin and end in the bedroom. She found the feel of the floor beneath her feet a sensual experience—a pleasant smell, an interesting texture in a fabric. She was more aware of the physical world around her.

Dominic took a deep breath and slowly released it. This was a strange sensation for him because while he was playing a minute ago, he had been thinking of Elle. His mind had been split. Part of it was down here translating the many emotions inside of him into music on the grand piano. Another part of him had been obsessing about Elle.

He'd wanted to be in bed with her, beside her, inside of her. Then he'd looked up and there she was, as if she'd materialized solely because he'd desired her so intensely.

"A few minutes," she answered him. "I didn't want you to stop."

When they reached each other, he pulled her into his arms. The thin fabric of the nightgown she wore was little hindrance to the pleasure he derived from running his hands over her back and bottom. "I was ready to stop for the night. I wanted to be upstairs with you." He breathed in her scent. "You smell so good." He kissed her cheek. "Why did you come downstairs?" he asked softly.

"I heard you playing and wanted to be closer to the music," she said. "To watch you play. I like watching you play."

Dominic bent and rained little kisses on her mouth, her chin, her throat as she tipped her head back to allow him easier access. Then he kissed her mouth, parting her lips and tasting her sweetness. Elle's arms went around his neck as she pressed her body closer to his, abrading her hardened nipples in the process.

"Mmm," Dominic moaned. He broke off the kiss to say hoarsely, as he gazed into her eyes, "Elle, there's something I want to ask you. Now, I don't expect you to answer right away. It's usually something a woman has to think about for a while. Weigh the consequences."

Oh, God, Elle thought. *Is he getting ready to propose?* Her heart thudded. She felt tingly with excitement all over. *Be calm, be calm*, she told herself.

"What is it?" she asked, her voice cracking in spite of attempts to sound normal and unperturbed.

Dominic smiled warmly and fondly touched her cheek. "I never thought I'd ask a woman to do this. I never thought I could bear to be around someone twenty-four hours a day and not wish for privacy. But with you I don't feel imprisoned. I crave your company. In fact, I think when you're around my work goes smoother. I feel inspired."

Elle felt like telling him, *Get on with it. Say the words!*

Looking into his eyes, though, she could tell that he was as excited by what he was about to say as she was.

He took both her hands in his, drew in a deep breath and said, "Elle, would you consider...living with me?"

Elle's mouth hung open in shock. She had to remind herself to close it, and then it closed with a soft pop! Live with him? Was he nuts? *She* believed in marriage and fidelity and having children. Perhaps he thought that because he had convinced her to enter into an affair with him when it was clearly against everything she believed in, she would take it one step further. In a Catholic country, for God's sake!

He interpreted her silence as surprise, not shock. He was still smiling at her. "I can see you have to think about it," he casually said as he picked her up and began walking to the stairs that led to their bedroom. "Take all the time you need. I'm in no rush, although I would like us to decide so that we can start looking for a house in Milan. I'm tired of apartment living. It's time to buy a home. Then we'll have a house in Milan where we can work all week, and come here on the weekends."

As she clung to him on the ride upstairs, Elle wanted to scream, *We'd just as well be married, you idiot! Living together, sleeping together, joined at the hip. We're already married!*

Inside, she was yelling like a banshee. Outside, she smiled calmly, her eyes looking into his as he carried her to their bed.

Then, as he set her down on the bed, a peaceful feeling came over her. Why was she getting upset? She had known what she was signing up for on opening night when she had agreed to be his lover. Dominic Corelli had a set of rules he lived by and he was oblivious to everything else.

She would think about his proposition. Yes, she would give it serious thought and if she decided that she just couldn't live with it, she would break it to him gently.

In the meantime, she would simply love him.

Chapter 15

Two weeks later they were back in Milan and Natalie had phoned and asked Elle to come to her yoga class with her. "It'll help you to relax between performances," she said, extolling the benefits of yoga. "And the breathing exercises are good for a singer. You'll be surprised by the extra lung capacity you'll gain. What do you say, Elle?"

Elle said yes.

So it was that after the first class, Natalie drove them to a little trattoria near Elle's apartment and they had lunch together. It was a beautiful fall day, and there wasn't a cloud in the crystalline blue sky. Elle couldn't appreciate it, though, because her mind was preoccupied with Dominic and his offer for her to live with him.

Natalie, looking wonderful in a black turtleneck and rust-colored slacks with matching suede boots, was chatting up a storm, not seeming to notice that Elle was very quiet. A nod of the head from Elle or a grunt seemed to satisfy her.

Then, after their meals were brought to their table and they'd picked up their forks to begin eating, Natalie dropped her fork back onto her plate with a clatter and cried, "What's going on with you, Elle? You have been so far away it's like I'm talking to a changeling."

"A changeling?" Elle asked.

"A child left on a human's doorstep by fairies. It was really a fairy disguised as a human. I don't remember why they did it, but that doesn't matter. The point is you look like Elle, but Elle is not here today!"

Elle focused. She smoothed her hair back. Recently she had started wearing it straight and, since the curls were relaxed, it now hung nearly to her waist. She had it in a ponytail today and was dressed in a chic black pantsuit and black leather boots.

Meeting Natalie's eyes across the table, she asked, "Are we friends?"

"You know I'm fond of you, Elle," Natalie said, a concerned expression bringing frown lines to her usually smooth forehead.

Elle smiled. "Yes, and I'm fond of you. But I need to know that we're true friends before I confide in you. This is not something I would normally talk to my boyfriend's mother about." Her eyes watered. "I have to make a decision and I'd like your opinion on it, if you can remain unbiased about it. No matter whom it concerns."

"This sounds serious," Natalie said. She liked Elle. She thought she was good for her son. That had been proven in so many ways since Dominic had started seeing her. He was calmer. He was actually happy. Not nearly as brooding as he used to be.

Natalie made up her mind. "I promise to be impartial, and to give you the best advice I can come up with. Tell me what's bothering you."

Elle took a deep breath. Looking Natalie straight in the eyes, she said softly, "Dominic asked me to move in with him."

A nerve underneath Natalie's right eye jumped. Elle could tell she wanted to say something but, to her credit, she didn't utter a word except to say, "Go on…"

"I know this sounds hypocritical," Elle said. "We're already lovers. Your family is well aware of it, so is my mother and my friends. But to me, moving in with a man feels like I'm giving up on ever having a real marriage, something secure, something I can count on, like you and Carlo have. And Dominic doesn't even seem to realize that's how I feel, when I've *told* him I want the traditional marriage with all the benefits."

Natalie nodded gravely. "I must say I'm with you. I was hoping for a wedding and, later on, babies. But at least my son is headed in the right direction with the right woman." She smiled. "Elle, you don't know how much he's changed since you've been in his life." She sighed. "He was so intense. He was like a caricature of a musical genius, caring only for his work. Oh, yes, he sincerely loves his family and he would do anything for us. But the women in his life were only accessories, Elle. None of them meant anything to him at all and they were interchangeable. Many of them were foreigners, living and working in Milan only for a while. He liked the fact that they would not always be here, just passing through."

"It was convenient for him," Elle surmised, "since he wasn't planning to invest his emotions in them anyway." Elle reminded herself that she was passing through, too.

"Exactly," said Natalie. She smiled at Elle. "When he brought you home to meet us, even though he swore that you were just his leading lady in the opera, I knew he was already half in love with you, Elle."

"He's not in love with me," Elle was quick to deny.

Still, deep down, she harbored hope that Natalie was right.

"Oh, but he is, my dear. I'm his mother, I know him. I might be wrong in saying this to you. I might be getting your hopes up that everything will turn out the way you want it to and Dominic will marry you. Then, if he doesn't, you'll be left brokenhearted, and I'll be left feeling guilty because I could have advised you to not go any further with this relationship. But I think you should follow your heart, Elle."

"But what will people say?"

Natalie laughed shortly. "It's 2010, Elle. Italian couples live together. Their mommas might not like it but it happens all the time. I can't say that Carlo won't give Dominic an earful, though. He believes that men should honor women with marriage if they're going to share their beds. I wouldn't be surprised if they haven't already had that conversation. But Carlo won't treat *you* any differently."

Elle thought about that. Carlo was always very sweet to her. She hated to disappoint him. She hated to disappoint herself. But maybe Natalie was right and Dominic was slowly warming to the idea of marriage.

"What are you going to do?" Natalie asked.

"I'm still thinking about it," Elle said truthfully.

Natalie picked up her fork. "Whatever you decide, I'm here for you. Now, let's eat before our food gets cold."

Later that night, Isobel disagreed with Natalie. "Don't do it. Sixty percent of couples who live together never get married. They either break up or wind up living together for years without the benefit of marriage. If you do it and you don't break up, how long do you think you'll stay with him before getting fed up? And what if you get pregnant? If he's okay with living with you without marrying you, doesn't it reason that he would also be perfectly happy to have a baby with you without getting married? One thing leads to another."

"I love him," Elle stated, just to put it on the table for Isobel to consider.

"Can't you love him without living with him?"

"Yes, but if this relationship is doomed anyway, I would prefer to spend as much time with him as possible before it's over."

"Do you know how desperate you sound?" Isobel asked, pulling no punches. "I didn't raise you to lower your standards in order to be with a man!"

"No, Isobel, you raised me to think independently. To know that, should the right man never ever come along, I would be fine on my own. And I know I will be fine after we're through, but for the first time in my life, I'm in love. And all of those feminist sayings about not needing a man don't resonate with me as much as they used to. Because unless you're in the thick of it, you really don't know how you're going to react. It sounds good to say I will never live with a man without the benefit of marriage, but the man I love is in the picture now and the fact of the matter is I would do anything to be with him."

Isobel sighed resignedly. "I hear you, baby. Just think about it a bit longer. Put on Aretha and have a glass of wine."

"You're not disappointed in me?" Elle asked.

"Hell, no," Isobel said with a laugh. "If anyone knows what it's like to be a fool for a man, it's your mother. I just hope you don't end up a bitter old woman like me."

"You're not a bitter old woman," Elle said firmly.

"I might not be old, but I'm definitely bitter," Isobel disagreed. She laughed again. "The stockbroker and I went out for coffee and, Elle, you wouldn't believe how hard he came on to me. Talk about lonely and desperate. He couldn't even wait until my coffee got cold before he was asking me to come back to his place with him. It seems that it's his theory that when men and women get to be a certain age they can skip the preliminaries and get right down to the dirty. And he thought I should have been grateful that he was showing me some attention. Grateful in the form of granting him sexual favors! You should have heard the string of cuss words at that table that day!"

"He has a filthy mouth on top of everything else?" Elle asked incredulously.

"No, I was the one cussing *him* out!" Isobel cried laughing. "Now when he sees me in the hallway he slinks in the other direction."

"See?" said Elle. "You don't have to worry about my getting hurt. Should worse come to worst between

Dominic and myself, I'll just cuss him out and go away and never see him again."

"Let's hope it'll be that easy," Isobel said.

Shortly after Elle and Dominic moved in together, she went to Madrid to star in Teatro Real's production of *Temptation*. Jaime reprised his role of Cristiano and on opening night it was as if all of Spain had come out to welcome their native son. The next morning, though, Elle got her share of rave reviews in the papers.

Meanwhile, Dominic was alone in their apartment in Milan, working on *Everlasting*, which was the new title of the opera he was composing.

One Saturday at around three in the afternoon, someone rang the bell and he got up from the piano to answer the door. He had on faded Levi's and a white T-shirt, his favorite lounging-around-the-house clothes, and he was barefooted.

A glance through the peephole revealed that it was Angelica calling. He had a visceral reaction to seeing her on the other side of his door. What was she doing here? He hadn't seen or called her in months, not since he had met Elle. What could she want? They had not had an understanding. He had not been expected to phone her and tell her he no longer wanted to see her. At least he didn't think he was expected to.

He stood silent at the door, wavering between pretending he wasn't at home and opening the door and greeting her warmly. After all, they were not enemies.

Of all the women he had slept with, he had always been sure of Angelica's detachment. She didn't love him any more than she loved that shiny sports car she tooled around Milan in. She used both for convenience—the car to get her from one place to another and him to satisfy her sexual needs.

So why was he hesitating to open the door?

She knocked this time instead of ringing the bell, and she pounded hard.

He took a deep breath and opened the door.

Angelica, all five feet three inches of her, fairly bristled with anger. She was a beautiful, voluptuous woman in her late twenties with long, sleek black hair, dark brown eyes, a full, sensuous mouth and a cute button nose. She exuded sexuality with every movement of her body. She understood the power a woman wielded with just a gesture, a glance, a whispered endearment. It was a practiced sexuality that she had learned in puberty and had been refining ever since. It had never failed her. Never, that is, until she realized Dominic was not ever going to phone her again for their Sunday-afternoon trysts. The first inkling she got was all the photos in the local papers of Dominic and Elle Jones. Then she had heard that they were seeing one another. That had not concerned her. Men often had their women at home and their women on the side. Then when he still didn't phone, she'd started to wonder—what was wrong with her that he would drop her, and the good thing they'd shared for the past three years, for a woman who wasn't half the woman she was?

That's when she'd started going places where she thought she might run into him, like Teatro alla Scala, in order to follow him home and confront him. For weeks, she had no luck. Then today she had seen him in a restaurant near here, where she had happened to be having a meal with another one of her male friends.

She had watched Dominic and, before he had finished his meal, she had ditched the friend she was with in order to be ready to roll when Dominic got up from his table.

She had been delighted to see he was walking. It might have been difficult to follow him if she'd had to hail a cab and yell, "Follow that car!"

But, no, he had walked only a few blocks to a well-maintained building and gone inside. At that point she'd lost her nerve and it had taken her two hours to work it up again. Then she had charmed the doorman into letting her come up.

"Aren't you going to invite me in?"

Dominic stood aside and she flounced into the apartment, her breasts jiggling in the bodice of her minidress. He shut the door but left it unlocked. With his back to the door, he watched as she walked into the apartment, assessing her surroundings. "Nice place," she said. She turned around and faced him, a false smile painted on her face. "Isn't that what a friend says when they see your place for the first time, since you never once invited me here?"

Dominic didn't crack a smile. He regarded her with narrowed eyes. Why was she so angry at him? "Forgive me, Angelica, but wasn't that part of the arrangement? I would come to you, you wouldn't come to me. Those were your stipulations. I saw no reason to give you my address. How did you get my address, anyway?"

"I have my ways," she said mysteriously. She walked up to him and stopped two feet away from him. "You could have phoned me and told me you weren't going to call me anymore. I haven't heard from you in seven months!"

Dominic's stony facade began to soften at the hurt tone in her voice. "I didn't think you expected me to say it was over."

"You thought I'd take the hint?" she asked.

"I didn't think you would care one way or the other. We weren't anything to each other except sexual partners. You often reminded me of that fact. You said you didn't want an emotional attachment and I told you I didn't either. Are you suddenly changing the rules because I stopped calling?"

Her face crumpled as tears began spilling from her eyes. "I said that because that's what I thought you wanted me to say!" she cried petulantly. "Even if I didn't care for you, Dominic, good manners dictate that you should at least send a note explaining why a relationship is being severed. In business or in personal affairs! You could have had the decency to call and leave me a message!"

Dominic reached out to comfort her by placing his hand on her arm, but she took the opportunity to leap into his arms and kiss him. Even though she was petite she was quite strong and clung to him like a leech.

Dominic roughly broke off the kiss. "Angelica, it's over. There, I'm telling you. It's over and you've got to get out of here," he said angrily. He tried to pry her arms from around his neck. She held on fast.

"Why?" she pleaded, tears leaving black mascara-laden streaks down her face. "Is *she* coming home soon? Come on, baby, let me make you feel good one last time and I'll be satisfied and never darken your door again."

Dominic didn't consider her offer for one second. He was already terrified that his nosy neighbor, Signora

Cimino, next door, would tell Elle she'd seen a strange woman going into their apartment. Signora Cimino, an opera purist, wasn't fond of *Temptation,* calling his mixture of classical and hip-hop music an abomination, but she allowed that even if the style was lacking, the substance that Elle brought to it had been wonderful. She'd become one of Elle's biggest fans and routinely plied her with fresh-baked pastries. However, whenever she saw Dominic she would shake her head pityingly and cluck her tongue. "I can't believe you have fallen so far. You've got everybody else fooled, but I know good opera and you, Maestro, have sold out."

"Look, Angelica," Dominic said now in an attempt to placate her, "don't do this. You deserve much better than I can give you. I'm sorry if I hurt you. It wasn't my intention. But I'm involved with someone else and I won't cheat on her."

Angelica suddenly screeched and let go of him. Her feet hit the floor with a thud and she pushed him hard against the chest, causing him to stumble backward. "I can't stand a reformed male whore!" she told him disdainfully. "You make me sick."

She walked to the door and looked back at him. "Next time, be careful how you treat people. No matter who we are, we deserve respect. I hope you treat her better than you did me, instead of using her for the next three years and then tossing her aside like so much trash. To hell with you, Dominic Corelli!"

She let out a breath as though she'd exorcised every bit of poison that she'd swallowed for the past seven months. She smiled as if she was somehow cleansed.

She pulled the door open and actually smiled at him when she turned back around, her hand on the doorknob. "It would be poetic justice if she broke your heart!"

She left then.

Dominic didn't move. He expected her to turn around and hurl expletives at him. But after two minutes passed, then three, he realized she'd gotten her feelings off her chest and wasn't coming back.

He went and locked the door. In spite of telling himself he hadn't done anything to deserve Angelica's wrath, he felt guilty. He strode through the apartment, back to the piano, where he sat down and began to play, but he couldn't concentrate.

Was he doing the same thing to Elle? Using her for his pleasure?

He told himself that was preposterous. He cared for Elle. It might seem cold-blooded, but he had never come close to feeling genuine affection for Angelica. From the moment they'd met in a bar he had known the score with her. Each of them had used the other. Then why had she come here today acting like a spurned lover?

Could Elle have been right when she had innocently told him that sex had consequences? Reasonably, he had to agree that she was. It was difficult to think of all the women he'd had casual affairs with and never given a second thought to when it was over. Had he left a string of Angelicas in his wake?

He didn't know. What he did know was that kind of behavior wouldn't be a part of his life anymore. He was happy with Elle. She was his equal in every way. It was easy to be faithful to her because all he wanted was her.

Fear suddenly clutched at him. That last invective Angelica had hurled at him—"It would be poetic justice if she broke your heart!" Was it possible that Elle would cheat on him? He didn't think so, but Angelica's words had put doubts in his mind.

Suddenly, he needed to get out of the apartment. He hurried into a pair of athletic shoes and grabbed his leather jacket from the closet near the door. He almost collided with Signora Cimino as she was walking to her apartment, her arms full of grocery bags.

"Here, let me help you," he said and held the bags for her while she rummaged in her voluminous purse for her apartment key.

She smiled at him and said, "Having Elle in your life has turned you into a gentleman, Signor Corelli. Don't do anything to mess it up."

She then took her bags and went inside without saying thank you.

Dominic laughed shortly, his mind momentarily off his paranoia. At least she hadn't been home when Angelica had visited. He didn't have her big mouth to worry about.

In December, Elle was home from a triumph in Madrid. They had learned that the cast album had been nominated for a Grammy Award and were planning to attend the ceremony in February.

They had just moved into their new house on the outskirts of Milan, not too far from Natalie and Carlo. Elle had been surprised by the swiftness with which Dominic had decided it was time to move from his old apartment. Dominic was glad that when Angelica had paid him a visit that day he and Elle hadn't already moved into their new home. Angelica wouldn't know where they lived now.

The house was what Dominic called a little villa. More than three thousand square feet of living space with marble floors, high ceilings, large rooms, a pool and a pool house in the back. Elle immediately fell in love with the kitchen because it was homey yet airy and opened onto the back garden, which was well kept and already had a vegetable garden that she was looking forward to replanting in the spring.

Upon her return from Madrid, Dominic couldn't help noticing that Elle looked somewhat fuller. He didn't know exactly how to describe it, but her breasts, already wonderful as far as he was concerned, were even more wonderful—rounder perhaps?

Her belly looked a bit rounder, too. He liked the way the extra weight made her look and he told her one day as they were showering together in the master bath.

Elle's eyes widened when he said it, which surprised him. But in an instant, she was smiling, so he put it out of his mind. "I guess I put on a few pounds in Madrid," she said lightly. She put her head under the shower's spray. She had tired of getting her naturally curly hair straightened and was back to her wavy style, which Dominic preferred.

Now he squeezed shampoo into his hand, rubbed it between his palms, then applied it gently to Elle's hair. He liked this part of their ritual. He loved her hair.

Elle luxuriated in the feel of his hands on her scalp. She'd never known a man who seemed to enjoy the sense of touch as much as Dominic did.

After she rinsed, he grabbed a towel and wrapped it turban-style around her head.

They got out of the shower, dried their bodies and

Elle went to the mirror to start drying her hair, with the diffuser on the hair dryer.

Dominic, a towel wrapped around his waist, stood in the doorway and watched her. He'd missed her when she had been in Madrid, but he had flown there to see her only once due to having to work himself. Besides, he didn't want to be a distraction to her when she was working. In almost a year, Elle had become a highly sought-after performer. She was solidly booked for the foreseeable future. He was proud of her.

She looked up and met his eyes in the mirror. "I love it when you watch me do mundane things like this," she told him, smiling. "It makes me think you must really, really like me to stand there and watch me dry my hair."

Finished, she bent and put the hairdryer under the sink, and before she could straighten back up, Dominic had her in his arms. "I do really like you." He crushed Elle to his chest and she winced. Dominic noticed and said, "What's wrong?"

Elle smiled, but it was forced, as he was well aware. "What?" she asked softly.

Dominic put a little space between them, but continued to firmly hold on to her. "Don't try to pretend you don't know what I'm talking about, Cara."

Elle smiled. "Okay, my breasts are a little sore."

Concern knitted Dominic's brows together. "Was I too rough last night?"

"No, I don't think it's that. Don't worry so much," Elle said dismissively. "Nothing is wrong with me that being with you won't fix." She tiptoed and briefly kissed his mouth. "Come on, now, we don't want to keep everybody waiting."

It was Sunday and they were due at his parents' villa for lunch.

When they got to his parents' home, Sophia and Matteo, who were newly engaged, were already there. Gianni and Francesca with little Gianni and his infant sister, Mia, arrived shortly after Dominic and Elle.

As it always happened, the small family behaved as if they hadn't seen each other in a very long time. There were warm hugs and kisses and delight expressed at small changes in each other.

Gianni, who hadn't seen Elle in a while, immediately noticed the change in her. He kept this observation to himself, though, and waited, thinking that there might be an announcement later on in the day.

After everyone had eaten and the ladies separated from the men as they usually did, he pulled Dominic aside in the study and asked, "How are you and Elle doing?"

Dominic smiled broadly. "Does this tell you anything?" he asked, referring to the wattage of his grin.

Yes, Gianni thought, *it tells me you are a fool, and what you don't know about women could fill the Colosseum in Rome.*

"It's going that well, huh?" Gianni said. He frowned. "If everything is so wonderful, why don't you marry her?"

Dominic, who was used to joking around with Gianni about his confirmed bachelorhood, laughed. "Why spoil a good thing? Elle and I are happy just the way things are."

Gianni wasn't smiling but Dominic was oblivious to this fact. "Are you sure Elle is happy the way things are?"

Dominic finally recognized the seriousness with

which his cousin was regarding him. "You're actually advising me to marry Elle?"

Gianni nodded gravely. "I am. I don't see why you won't. For all intents and purposes you're already married, except for making it legal." He sighed. "No, cousin, I'm going to be brutally honest with you—living together is nothing like marriage. When you live with someone you can leave whenever you want with no strings attached, least of all emotional ties. That's not love. With marriage, you make a commitment to stay together through bad times and good times. When you marry someone you're telling the world that you love and respect this person and you will do everything in your power to be there for her always. Living together is just a convenience. And I think you care more for Elle than to make her a convenience!"

To hear his cousin, whom he loved as a *fratello,* refer to him as little more than a user upset Dominic. Especially on top of the things Angelica had said to him a few weeks ago. To his shame, though, he stubbornly clung to the belief that he and Elle were fine and what had happened between him and Angelica could never happen between him and Elle.

He was angry with his cousin for trying to tell him how to live his life. "How dare you accuse me of using Elle?" he shouted, standing up and pacing the room.

His cousin looked hurt by his tone of voice, but Dominic didn't care. Gianni had hurt him, too, by speaking so frankly about a touchy subject.

"I'm actually happy for the first time in a long time. Why do you begrudge me my happiness?" Dominic asked angrily.

Gianni was not one to back down from a fight.

He faced him, his dark eyes defiant and his stance belligerent. "You're behaving like your actions have no consequences. That's blindly irresponsible. Be a man, Dominic. Grow up!"

"Don't tell me to grow up," Dominic ground out between clenched teeth. "It was Elle's choice to live with me. I'm not forcing her to stay."

"No," Gianni agreed. "All you used was gentle persuasion on a young woman whose experience in these things is far less than yours!"

"Keep your voice down!"

"I will not keep my voice down!"

Dominic hit him on the jaw. Gianni stumbled backward but didn't fall. He and Dominic were fairly equally matched in height and weight, although Dominic had more muscle mass due to his weight-lifting regimen.

Gianni hit him back, harder.

Dominic's hand went to his split lip. He looked down at the blood on his hand. "What's gotten into you? You're acting crazy."

"I'm going to beat some sense into you," Gianni yelled and leaped onto Dominic. They both went down onto the Persian carpet in the study and overturned the heavy coffee table in front of the leather couch.

"Stop this at once!" Carlo yelled at his son and nephew as he came running into the room, Matteo and the women on his heels.

He got between the combatants and held them apart. Out of respect for him, neither his son nor his nephew continued to try to get at each other around him. "What's this all about?" Carlo demanded, looking first at Dominic, then at Gianni. "You two haven't had a brawl since you were schoolboys."

Dominic and Gianni's eyes shot daggers at one another but both refused to talk.

Elle moved around the group of women and Matteo to go to Dominic. Seeing her calmed him down and he let go of the anger. He turned toward her and she reached up to gently touch his split lip. Dominic stood there, looking down into her concerned eyes. He adored her. He adored her and he wanted her in his life forever.

He pulled her into his arms. Looking deeply into her eyes, he whispered, "*Tesoro mio,* are you unhappy with me?"

Elle tensed. The entire family was watching her and Dominic with intense interest. She had heard only the tail end of the argument. Why had the cousins bloodied each other's faces? Dominic was bleeding from the mouth, and Gianni from the nose.

Now he was asking her if she was unhappy with him. "Can't we go somewhere private?" she asked, her eyes pleading with him to agree.

Dominic shot an angry glance at Gianni. "No, please, I want everyone to hear. Some people believe I've disrespected you somehow by asking you to live with me. I want them to hear your opinion on the subject."

Carlo stepped forward. "Dominic, can't you see you're embarrassing Elle?"

"Elle is a part of this family," Dominic insisted. "She should feel free to say anything in your presence."

Elle suddenly felt nauseous. Now that she thought of it, there had been cheese in the salad today, and lately dairy foods hadn't been agreeing with her. Plus, the stress Dominic was putting on her by wanting to discuss their private business in front of his family wasn't helping.

Her stomach contracted painfully, and bile rose in her throat. With one hand on her midsection and the other over her mouth, she turned from Dominic and muttered, "I don't feel well."

Gianni whispered to Francesca, "Go with her. I think Elle is expecting."

Shocked, Francesca said aloud, "Expecting!"

Everyone heard. Elle was mortified. She ran from the room. Francesca took off behind her, only to be overtaken by Dominic, who grabbed her by the arm and said, "Let me go with her."

Francesca went back into the study, where everyone was staring at one another with confused expressions.

"I knew she was absolutely glowing!" was Natalie's comment.

"Our first grandchild," Carlo said wistfully, smiling broadly.

Sophia laughed. "I hope it's going to be triplets. Dominic and his plans—little did he realize that God had a bigger plan for him!"

Chapter 16

Elle ran to the hall bathroom and tried to close and lock the door before Dominic elbowed his way in, but he was too fast for her. "If there is any time I would prefer to be in a bathroom by myself, this is it!" she cried. But that was all she had time to say before she was on her knees and throwing up into the commode.

Dominic got a washcloth from the linen shelf, ran warm water over it, wrung it out and handed it to her as she flushed. Elle accepted it, wiped her mouth, closed the lid of the toilet and sat down on it. She felt a lot better after purging.

The smell was horrendous. She looked up at Dominic. "Please leave me to my humiliation."

Dominic sat down on the edge of the tub and reached for her hand. Looking at her with nothing but love in his eyes, he asked softly, "When were you going to tell me?"

"Maybe never," Elle admitted.

Dominic let that sink in a moment. "That means you were planning to leave me before you started showing more than you already are." He realized now that the extra weight, the enhanced breasts, were due to Elle's pregnancy. "I've been such a fool."

"No more than I've been," Elle said softly with a gentle smile. "I should have told you as soon as I found out, but I was afraid you would accuse me of trying to trap you into marriage, which wasn't my intention."

"The blame is mine," Dominic told her, his eyes caressing her face. "I should have been more diligent about the condoms. You warned me."

Elle laughed shortly as she lowered her gaze. "Yes, I did, didn't I? But you can't take all the blame. I should have made sure you used a condom. There were times I simply felt like letting go and forgetting to be responsible."

Dominic lifted her chin so that she was looking into his eyes. "Lately, things have been happening that have made me rethink my life." He briefly told her about his encounter with Angelica, and what the argument between him and Gianni had been about. "I couldn't bear it if I lost you." His eyes were misty. "It breaks my heart that you were thinking of never telling me about the bambino, *tesoro*. Don't you know I adore you?"

Sniffing, Elle said, "You put on a pretty good act of not wanting a commitment."

Dominic laughed regretfully. "A man says a lot of things he doesn't mean."

He bent his head to kiss her and Elle drew back. "Trust me on this, you don't want to kiss me until I brush and gargle."

Dominic pulled her up and hugged her tightly instead. After which he gazed down at her. "When we're married, I get to kiss you whenever I want to, okay?"

Elle's heart leaped with joy. "Okay!"

When Elle emerged from the bathroom she found the entire family waiting for her. Dominic immediately pulled her into his arms and kissed her soundly. Then he announced, "I asked Elle to marry me and she took pity on me and said yes."

Cheers filled the cramped hallway and after jubilant hugs and kisses, they went to the kitchen, where Carlo produced a bottle of champagne he kept in the fridge just for such occasions. He popped the cork and everyone drank to Elle and Dominic's happiness. Elle was provided with a glass of juice.

Natalie couldn't help continually hugging her soon-to-be daughter-in-law. "Oh, Elle, I keep going back to that day in the café when you asked for my advice about Dominic. I couldn't be happier that it turned out the way we wished it would. I love you like a daughter."

"I love you, too," Elle assured her with a happy smile.

Later, Elle phoned her mother with the news and was given some news herself. Isobel and John had gotten married in Vegas. Elle jokingly asked if her mother was pregnant and Isobel cried, "The only thing I'm expecting is to be happy."

Dominic and Elle were married in late August. Elle had three bridesmaids, Belana, Patrice and Ana; and two maids of honor, Francesca and Sophia, who had married Matteo in May. She was noticeably pregnant, which she and Elle joked about because Elle had waited to marry Dominic so that she wouldn't be pregnant while walking down the aisle. Baby Ariana was only a month and a half and already spoiled by everyone in both families. She could not whimper without someone running to pick her up and give her some love, especially her father, who wondered how he could have lived all his life without someone this precious to cuddle.

Elle's new stepfather, John, gave her away. When she had asked him, he had shyly accepted, saying that he considered her his daughter and it was nice that she felt the same about him. And Elle did. She was so happy that her mother had found a good man, someone who would treat her well and always stand by her.

Gianni was Dominic's best man and several of his cousins were his groomsmen.

On the day of the wedding, it rained in the morning but stopped at midday and, by the time the guests had arrived, the sun had nearly dried up the rain on the ground. The garden was a lush paradise. Chairs had been set up on either side of the aisle, which had a deep red runner down it. White roses adorned the chairs on the aisle and the wedding canopy.

Dominic and Gianni were already under the canopy by the time the music began playing, and everyone drew in a surprised breath when Natalie rose and sang an aria in honor of her son and his new wife. Not a dry eye was to be seen when she finished. The diva still had it. She moved to sit in the front row beside her husband, who was wiping a tear from his eye. *"Bellissima, cara mia,"* he told her as he kissed her cheek.

The processional music began to play and the

bridesmaids and groomsmen walked down the aisle arm in arm. The bridesmaids wore sophisticated designer gowns in deep colors. Elle hadn't wanted pastels at her wedding. The groomsmen wore traditional black tuxedos.

The wedding march began and Elle was escorted down the aisle by John, who was also wearing a tuxedo. All eyes were on the bride, though, who wore a one-of-a-kind empire-waist gown with a beaded, silver bodice and a cream-colored, silk brocade skirt. It was exquisitely beautiful. However, the bride outshone her apparel. Elle glowed with the assurance of the love surrounding her. In a few minutes she would be united with the only man she had ever loved in holy matrimony.

When Dominic saw his bride, his heart was full. He had almost lost her, this unique woman. What would he have done without her?

Once Elle's hand was in his and they were standing in front of all of their loved ones, a peaceful feeling descended upon him and he realized that this was what life was all about. It wasn't how famous you could become, or how rich you could become that mattered. To be rich in love was his goal from now on.

After he and Elle said their vows and the priest pronounced them husband and wife, he kissed his new bride. When he lowered his head and looked down into her upturned face, he said, *"Ti amo, ora e per sempre."*

Later the photographer took pictures of the wedding party. Elle's favorite was the one in which she and Dominic were standing side by side and he was holding Ariana in his arms, peering into her little face. Looking up at her father, Ariana was making happy noises and blowing spit bubbles.

After Ariana was put down for a nap, Elle and Dominic sat enjoying a light meal at the reception, which was held in the garden. White-linen-topped tables with floral centerpieces dotted the flagstone patio. A gentle breeze was coming off the lake and the August sky was clear of clouds. In the background, a string quartet played the classics.

At Dominic and Elle's table, Gianni had risen and was making a toast. "To Elle and Dominic—may they have a long, happy marriage and be blessed with many bambinos!"

"Sì, sì," said Carlo, touching champagne flutes with his wife on his right. "Your mother and I love being grandparents. Ariana has only whetted our appetites for more."

Dominic laughed. "Sophia and Matteo will be adding to the family very soon. As for Elle and I, we're going to simply enjoy Ariana for a while. My leading lady has agreed to star in *Everlasting* and has to maintain her splendid figure."

Elle looked lovingly into her husband's eyes. She had the best of both worlds: a career she loved and a husband who fully supported her. She couldn't have been happier.

She rose. "I have a couple of friends to thank for convincing me to come to Italy with them." She smiled at Belana and Patrice. "I might still be in the chorus if not for you two. Thank you, I'll always be grateful."

"Now that we're stepsisters," Belana told her, grinning, "I feel free to tell you that it's been my pleasure over the years to bully you into doing what's best for you. But the fact is, Elle, if you didn't have the talent to back up our bullying, you would still be in the chorus!"

Everyone laughed.

Patrice gently tapped her champagne flute with a fork, getting everyone's attention. She cleared her throat because she felt tears were imminent. "We've been like sisters since Juilliard. I have to admit, while I'm extremely happy for you, Elle, I'm going to miss you like crazy. With you here in Italy, Belana in New York and me in Los Angeles, when are we going to see each other?"

The three friends wound up in a group hug, whispering reassurances of their continued loyalties. Tears flowed freely.

John and Isobel went to them and offered sympathy. "Come now, girls," said Isobel gently. "This isn't the end, this is the beginning. Perk up!"

Elle, Patrice and Belana looked at each other and burst into laughter. "Look at us," Elle said, "behaving like crybabies." She hugged Patrice. "I'm only a phone call away, Miss Hollywood. You're going to be too busy working on that new T. K. McKenna movie to worry about me." Then she pulled Belana into her arms. "And as for you, stepsister, New York City hasn't yet seen the best you have to give. You're going to take it by storm. Now I'm going to dance with my husband."

Dominic, who had been watching with a smile playing at the corners of his generous mouth, got up and pulled her into his arms.

Then he took his bride onto the dance floor and they danced the first dance of the rest of their lives together.

Common Italian Words and Phrases

A domani—See you tomorrow

Bella—beautiful

Bellissimo(a)—Very beautiful

Benvenuto—welcome

Buon giorno—good morning; good day

Buona notte—good night (said when someone is retiring for the night.)

Cara mia—my darling

Ciao—hello, or goodbye

Come stai?—How are you?

Fratello—brother

Grazie—Thank you

Mi scusi—Excuse me

Molte grazie—Thank you very much

Ora e per sempre—now and forever
Sì—Yes
Tesoro mio—my treasure
Ti amo—I love you
Uno fiasco—an utter failure

* * * * *

REQUEST YOUR FREE BOOKS!

2 FREE NOVELS
PLUS 2 **FREE GIFTS!**

KIMANI™
ROMANCE

Love's ultimate destination!

THE *MATCH MADE* SERIES

Melanie Harte's exclusive matchmaking service—
The Platinum Society—can help any soul find their
ideal mate. Because when love is perfect,
it is a match made in heaven...

Book #1
by *Essence* Bestselling Author
ADRIANNE BYRD
Heart's ♥ Secret
June 2010

Book #2
by National Bestselling Author
CELESTE O. NORFLEET
Heart's ♥ Choice
July 2010

Book #3
by *Essence* Bestselling Author
DONNA HILL
Heart's ♥ Reward
August 2010

www.kimanipress.com
www.myspace.com/kimanipress

KPMMSP